PEPPERPOT

Best New Stories from the Caribbean

PEEKASH PRESS

This collection is comprised of works of fiction. All names, characters, places, and incidents are the product of the authors' imaginations. Any resemblance to real events or persons, living or dead, is entirely coincidental.

Published by Peekash Press
©2014 Peekash Press

US (Akashic) ISBN-13: 978-1-61775-271-1
UK (Peepal Tree) ISBN: 978-1-84523-237-5
Library of Congress Control Number: 2013956050

Peekash Press (US office)
c/o Akashic Books
PO Box 1456, New York, NY, 10009, USA
www.akashicbooks.com

Peekash Press (UK office)
c/o Peepal Tree Press
17 King's Avenue, Leeds LS6 1QS, United Kingdom
www.peepaltreepress.com

TABLE OF CONTENTS

PART III: MIND GAMES

Introduction

The seed that grew Peekash Press was sown when the CaribLit project, supported by Commonwealth Writers and the British Council, invited Johnny Temple of Akashic Books and Jeremy Poynting of Peepal Tree Press to attend the Kingston Book Festival in January 2013. Over a few beers, we agreed to work together to deliver commitments made at an earlier meeting held in Port of Spain in 2012, as an adjunct to the NGC Bocas Lit Fest. This was to support the growth of a regional literary infrastructure, including publishing. Both Akashic and Peepal Tree have fine lists of Caribbean fiction and poetry, but we acknowledged that writers based in the Caribbean are less likely to be published than those living in the British or North American diasporas.

Both Akashic Books and Peepal Tree Press will continue with our separate commitments to publishing the best Caribbean writing, new and classic, but we agreed to set up a joint imprint specifically dedicated to new writers within the region. With the assistance of Kellie Magnus as convener of CaribLit, a competition was run to come up with a name for the joint imprint—and amongst other good suggestions, *Peekash* was the one we all liked best. It sounded like something you could eat—something a little spicy, but nourishing. Many of the other names suggested were specific to individual islands, and this insularity suggests one of the barriers to the creation of a cross-Caribbean literary market. But as Olive Senior's lovely preface on page 11 argues, it is a wholly artificial barrier, where under the surface of a delightful linguistic diversity, the unity, as Kamau Brathwaite long ago insisted, is submarine.

This is why *Pepperpot*, an anthology of the best stories from the 2013 Caribbean entries for the Commonwealth Short Story Prize, is such a good fit. Whilst there are countries missing from the selection—we went for quality not token representation—it does have the beginnings of a cross-Caribbean mix, and we hope it will range even wider next year. The chance to look at a good number of the almost two hundred entries to the competition gave a rewarding glimpse into the current preoccupations of Caribbean writers; it confirmed the reputation of a number of already published authors, and revealed some exciting new talents. The gaps point to one of the challenges for CaribLit and Commonwealth Writers—how to support those countries whose writers don't feature in the anthology, where the issue of size is often pertinent.

Whilst for logistical reasons this first Peekash Press publication has been handled by Akashic and Peepal Tree, it is our intention that, over time, editorial input to Peekash Press will shift to the region. As Peekash's founders, we hope that in time the press will become autonomous, and able to choose what its relationship to us will be. How this will happen will be a topic for future discussion.

The Partners:

Commonwealth Writers is the cultural initiative of the Commonwealth Foundation. It inspires, develops, and connects writers and storytellers in a range of disciplines. It then links them to groups which seek to bring about social change.
www.commonwealthwriters.org

CaribLit is a local economic development initiative committed to strengthening literary culture, publishing, and related activities in the Caribbean. It is currently supported by Commonwealth Writers in partnership with the British Council.
www.CaribLit.com

NGC Bocas Lit Fest, now in its fourth year, is directed by Marina Salandy-Brown, with Nicholas Laughlin as programme manager. This festival was one of the founding partners of the original Caribbean Literature Action Group. Appropriately, *Pepperpot* will be launched at Bocas 2014.
www.bocaslitfest.com

Akashic Books is the Brooklyn-based publishing house whose vibrant Caribbean list features writers such as Colin Channer, Marlon James, Elizabeth Nunez, Robert Antoni, and Anthony C. Winkler, among many others. The Caribbean is well represented in its location-based Noir Series (*Kingston Noir*, *Trinidad Noir*, *Haiti Noir*, etc.).
www.akashicbooks.com

Peepal Tree Press is a Leeds (UK) publishing house with around three hundred Caribbean titles on its list. It is the publisher of the Caribbean Modern Classics series. Its authors Kendel Hippolyte and Rupert Roopnaraine were, respectively, the winners of the 2013 Bocas poetry and nonfiction prizes.
www.peepaltreepress.com

Preface
by Olive Senior

One thing that unites us in the Caribbean is food, especially the melange: we all love pepperpot by any name—calalu or sancocho or "Saturday soup." Ivory Kelly could be talking about this collection of stories when (in "This Thing We Call Love") she writes, "My mother and her friends' conversations were like boil-up, with plantains and cassava and other kinds of ground food and salted meat thrown into a pot of water, in no particular order, and boiled until the pot is a steaming, bubbling, savoury cuisine."

The mixture in this *Pepperpot* might be more formal than a boil-up, as befits two excellent publishers coming together, but their new imprint serves up a tasty and satisfying meal: familiar and high-quality ingredients with just a touch of that indefinable "something" in the mix to make it tempting, challenging, and, ultimately, satisfying.

This volume represents the culmination of a dream of book lovers and creators throughout the Caribbean to find ways to share our words with each other as well as with those beyond our shores. Now Peekash is here to "break down barriers of insularity and create a pan-Caribbean market," as the sponsors Peepal Tree Press and Akashic Books have declared.

The latter should be made easier by the manner in which this first collection of stories already speaks in a Caribbean voice, one that is elusive yet ever-present. These stories share enough common ground to enable any Caribbean reader to identify with the characters and situations described, even if the settings and the specific events or ways of life might be beyond their immediate experience.

Overall, the descriptions and images used in each story contribute to a Caribbean cultural mosaic in subtle, unstated ways that transcend speech. The non-Belizean reader might not know exactly what the purchaser will get at the "panades" shop when he or she asks for "two dollars salbutes and a dollar garnaches," but from the setting, tone, and robust vitality of the actors at the food stand, we can simply substitute in our minds doubles, bakes, or fritters.

National origins do not shout but quietly reveal themselves through subtle codes or gestures that speak of the particular. In Barbara Jenkins's "A Good Friday," we know we are in Trinidad when the noisy domino players consume Stag beer and the scarlet ibis is the motif of the mosaic tabletop, but the story itself would work just as well in any of the islands. And while "red Chinese-Payol-African mix-up creole skin" are not the words a Jamaican or Bahamian writer might use, we would have no difficulty in seeing the character described and substituting words from our own lexicon.

This feeling of familiarity is what delights, in a collection that ranges from Belize to the Bahamas, Antigua, Trinidad, Barbados, and Jamaica. We can enter each narrative and find enough that is familiar to feel instantly at home. Browsing *Pepperpot* is like overhearing family *sus* about relatives we have never met but who are nevertheless part of our bloodlines: like the great-uncle who fathered "plenty-plenty" children including some in foreign lands when he worked on the Panama Canal, or the persistent whispers that a beloved "daughter" is really a grandchild, born to a daughter whose shame had to be hidden. We know about getting something to "tie" lovers and how such trafficking with the occult can rebound; about the dangers to small children of Ol'Higue and her "sweet mouth" and how strange, mysterious traps lurk for those who aren't extra careful in reading the signs on Good Friday. Above all, we know that terrible, dark stains can lurk in families, as they do in the wider society, and that money and status are no shields from pain and exploitation.

These are just some of the issues explored in the following pages. The stories veer between dark and light, run between the shadows and the sun, assuming playful ol'talk or inscribing the screams of the dying. The way they play out might be identified with a particular island and its current ethos, but the larger issues raised are universal. They have the authentic feel of writers with their feet firmly planted in the place they are writing about.

The stories are for the most part serious but, like Caribbean life, are often salted and spiced with humour and the sweetness of island expressions. Whether probing family secrets, interrogating attitudes to intolerance of difference, or wrestling with issues of justice, religion, and moral values in a violent world, there is nothing here that should strike a Caribbean reader as strange or odd or untrue, because each story is engaged in finding coping strategies in a world that is not ordered but serves as a testing ground for the individual.

Family relationships are big in these stories—families on the way to healing or disintegration. Or with no family values at all, as when "waywardness" is inbred in the fabric of a society which then blames the victim. "I call him Brian but you can call him anything you please," Ezekel Alan says of his harrowing inner-city everyman.

Similarity and difference sometimes walk hand in hand: Garfield Ellis's "Father, Father" unravels with the intensity of a Greek tragedy, while Kevin Jared Hosein's "The Monkey Trap" runs just as inevitably but on the slow and mournful cadence of a daughter's sorrowful love for her father, or, as in "Berry" (Kimmisha Thomas), a woman's love for another. Dwight Thompson's "The Science of Salvation" raises serious questions of faith and redemption while Sharon Millar's protagonist in "The Whale House" seeks release from the weight of family lies and secrets.

There are stories here that purely delight and stories that ask more serious questions of the individual and society, involving the reader in the moral questions embedded in the quest for justice. One might see many of these stories as revenge tragedies with different outcomes played out on each island stage. From the complex Sukiya enacting her sweet revenge in Kevin Baldeosingh's contemporary "Cheque Mate" to Sharon Leach's harrowing, twisted tale of incest and vengeance ("All the Secret Things No One Ever Knows").

On the other side is the search for redemption, for righting the wrongs of history. Several writers resort to fantasy or speculative fiction as if to seek assurance that justice will be done. For the reader, as for the narrators, traditional folklore provides a sort of comforting balm to ease the pain of those afflicted and turns the world right-way-up again. While the stories do not go so far, we know from our own knowledge that Ol'Higue will always perish for her misdeeds (Janice Lynn Mather's "Mango Summer") and, like the "singing bone" of legend, the dead girl in the end will be accorded justice and the wicked punished (Joanne C. Hillhouse's "Amelia at Devil's Bridge"). More troubling is the possible outcome in Heather Barker's fantasy melding biblical history and contemporary Barbados ("And the Virgin's Name Was Leah") because it subverts so much of our prior knowledge and expectations.

The stories aim for an authentic rendering of Caribbean people and events from the inside, and so in the landscapes of *Pepperpot* we find none of the stereotyped sea and beach idylls of the tourist brochures. Here in the rocky haunts of the islanders themselves are landscapes where "the rocks are sharper than a coconut vendor's cutlass, and the waters lash with a vengeance," landscapes of swollen gullies and bush where monkeys can hide, where beauty and violence compete in scorpion fish and stingrays and captured, gutted shark. There are also the landscapes where lush fruit falls to the ground with the ease of summer ripening, where the clash of dominoes in the rum shop provides the familiar auditory signal of men at play, and where preachers get the urge to go into the streets and warn of coming tribulations even as gunshots spatter.

These are true, authentic voices speaking in a variety of tones, cadences, and rhythms, hiding nothing, releasing images that will continue to haunt us long after we have closed the book. Spoken in tones that are musical, mildly satirical, or hauntingly lyrical, cutting across various speech registers, allowing us to hear our own voices calling to one another.

Pepperpot is the start of what we hope will be the creation of solid pan-Caribbean publishing of creative work. Peekash has hung out its sign. Waiting for the clientele to enter, enjoy, and beg for more. Let's line up and support it.

PART I

Love & Theft

SHARON MILLAR

The Whale House
Trinidad & Tobago

These offshore islands rise out of the water, rugged and black with deep crevices and craggy promontories. Her father used to tell the story of building the house. Dynamite under the water to blow a hole in the hill, a false plateau appearing like a shelf, the hill buckled up behind it. Sometimes after heavy rain, stones clatter lightly on the roof as the soil shifts and moves behind the house. Her parents' ashes are buried here in the rocky, flinty soil, but Laura and Mark scatter the baby's ashes in the ocean, looking for black-finned porpoises as the talcum-powder dust hovers on the misty spray. When Mark releases the last of the ashes they drive the boat toward the house in silence. Laura is the first to slip over the side, wading carefully toward the shore, eyes on the horizon. Over the years she's learned to watch for scorpion fish and the low-lying stingrays that rise like illusions when dusk slides into the bay.

Mark had cried in the hospital, but now, after they've scattered the ashes, there's just the heat of blame rising off him. Even in the boat, he'd passed her with averted eyes. Later that night, she waits for him on her side of the two single beds pushed together. But by the time he comes up from the jetty she is already dreaming hard. Under the sepia mosquito net, she lies on her side, a small feather pillow between her legs. The mosquitoes settle in dark clumps on the netting, whining softly into the night air.

By morning the dreams are gone, flying through the tiny holes in the net in sudden starling movements. The twin beds are pushed together and the net strains to cover both of them. She wakes with the mist of the dreams still heavy in the room and moves up behind her husband, trying to wrap her body around his larger one. To reach him she must lie on the join in the bed. The hard knotted bump where the mattresses meet bites into her hip, but she lies still, matching her breathing to his soft exhalations; when she feels his breathing change, she knows he's awake. Overnight their legs have tangled, their limbs sealing in the humidity, but slowly he inches his leg away with the soft mollusk sound of flesh separating. She rolls back over onto her side and he leaves the room without speaking.

Would the baby have survived if she'd rested in the afternoons, stayed in bed as the doctor had advised? Mark has not accused her of endangering the baby. Such a bald statement would take them to a dangerous edge. So instead it is hovering between them, nebulous and monstrous. She had not rested enough, she knows, but it had been a time of neither wanting nor not wanting, a strangely remote period. It is that indifference that she is exploring, testing it as gently as a tongue on a wound. She'd thought the feeling hidden, so solidly concealed that she'd doubted its potency. But now there is no baby, the grief has come upon her, making her bones hollow..

Out the window, the tide is changing, the sea frothing and roiling into the tight channel. But beyond, in the harbor, it expands in relieved swells, glad to be past the slick mountain walls. Four months ago, Laura had gone to see Dr. Harnaysingh. She'd made the appointment because at forty-six, her body was suddenly an unknown entity. Once calm and predictable, a source of surety and absolutes, it was now dense, fleshy, prone to thickened skin and odd middle-aged lust. She'd missed three periods, but pregnancy was not something she'd considered. She'd been researching menopause and hormone-replacement options. When she'd told Mark, he lifted her nightie, rested his dark head between her ribs and hip bones, and traced gentle circles around the hard space above her pubic bone. She'd imagined a light swooping and fluttering deep inside of her as Mark murmured to the quicksilver heartbeat, that mere conspiracy of cells. A baby.

The day she'd felt the new baby's first movements, she cracked three eggs. She separated the yolks from the whites; each yellow globe quivering gently on the edge of a shell as the clear albumin streamed into the bowl. Alone, in their blue bowl, the yolks leaned into one another, separated by the thinnest of membranes. Gently she skewered them, holding the bowl tightly to gain purchase on the slippery surface. When she next saw Dr. Harnaysingh, she lied, smoothly and easily, assuring him that she was being careful and staying off her feet. At home, she continued to bake cakes, casseroles, soufflés; balancing on the stepladder as she lugged down heavy iron pots and ancient mixing bowls. She even weeded the back stairs, squatting heavily on the mossy concrete, the varicose veins in her ankles thudding in protest.

"Shouldn't you be resting more?" Mark asked.

The baby was born at just twenty-eight weeks.

"Come, baby, breathe," Dr. Harnaysingh said.

Mark sat in the corner of the room, his head in his hands. Laura stretched the lavender baby along the inside of her arms, the perfect feet pressing against her breasts, the heels of her hands supporting the fragile head. Cupping the tender skull with both hands, she kissed the violet fingers, ears, and toes, running her fingers along the butterfly eyebrows. To keep her warm she pulled the baby close to her breast, swaddling and rocking her. After three hours, Dr. Harnaysingh sedated her so they could pry the baby from her.

"Can babies feel regret?" Laura asked Dr. Harnaysingh as the opiate dripped into her veins.

Now the ashes have sunk to the bottom of the sea, Mark is downstairs; the musical sound of his spoon beating the cup. The room Laura lies in faces the sea. It was her parents' room. Her father built four rooms, three that face the sea and a smaller one that looks into the flinty soil of the hill. The small room is the nursery with its tiny cots and miniature bunks. When the children were little, she often woke in the night panicked that the toddlers had been swept away in the night currents. A neighbour deeper in the bay had lost a two-year-old that way, the child climbing out of his crib and making his way down the stairs and over the jetty. In those days, Laura's stairs had had two wrought-iron gates, one at the top and one at the bottom, each padlocked with a little gold key.

From the window she sees Jeannine on the jetty. It still surprises her that this is her firstborn. There is an old photograph of Laura holding Jeannine and smiling at the camera. The caption reads: *What a great big sister! Monos, 1982.* She's sure her parents suspected she was sleeping with Mark, but what could they do? It had only stopped when they'd been caught. But by that time she was already pregnant. A small copse of trees runs down the hill stopping before the jetty. Does her mother's plot with medicinal herbs still exist? If her mother were alive, she would know what poultices to place on Laura's aching breasts. She'd had one for a cough and one to lower blood pressure. But Laura only remembers the one meant to flush a womb and make the blood run red and clean. Its romantic name conjured crystal lights and grown-up parties that made you forget the spiky vicious head and bitter green stems. Chandelier bush. A strong brew could make a womb vomit a baby. It's good for cramps, her mother had said. It will help bring down a reluctant period. Clean you out good and proper. But it had not worked because Laura learned to hold the noxious green tea in her mouth until she could spit it out. The period never came. You have your whole life ahead of you, her mother said. Drink it. But she didn't.

Her own teenagers are downstairs now. Aidan is seventeen; Sonia, nineteen. Aidan's girlfriend, Ivy, honey-coloured and wholesome, is there as well. They are baking a cake for her, to cheer her up. Later they will all walk to the other side of the island for a swim. When she turned sixteen, her mother baked a cake and gave her a ruby ring, July's birthstone. Mark left for school that September. Laura had been due to go as well but all that had been cancelled. Her mother was only forty-six, still young enough to have a baby and heavy enough that no one doubted the pregnancy. Her father had closed his practice and taken up a temporary locum job in St. Kitts, moving the family there until Jeannine was born. Her mother delivered Jeannine in Laura's bedroom. Laura laboured for a full day and a night on the flowered shower curtain that her mother placed below her, the pains sawing her until she split in two with Jeannine, as the baby slipped into her mother's waiting hands. Now there were two of them. In that small room so long ago, she'd seen her mother's face change as she held Jeannine, seen the longing.

Once, years later, after Mark and Laura were married, they'd gone to Tobago on holiday. Sonia and Aidan were little things. They'd stopped at the famous mystery tomb of twenty-three-year-old Betty Stivens. *She was a mother without knowing it, and a wife without letting her husband know it, except by her kind indulgences to him. 1783.* What does that mean, Mummy? Sonia asked her again and again. Could you be my mother and not know it? No, baby, of course not. That's why it's a mystery tomb. But she couldn't get Betty Stivens out of her mind. Maybe she had not been as lucky as Laura, had not had a doctor as a father and a nurse as a mother. Maybe she'd never lived to see the child. Maybe she'd laboured to death in some dark room on her own. It's like a riddle, she'd said to Sonia, and no one knows what it really means.

Mark never knew. Only Laura had been left with her split self and a new sibling. By the time he'd come back, it was too late to tell him. How could she? And how could they take Jeannine from her parents? Even after she'd had Sonia, then Aidan, she still glanced at Jeannine out of the corners of her eyes. When her parents were killed in an accident, coming home after a weeknight Chinese meal, it was all too late to tell. Now she is the only one who knows.

Later that morning, they walk to the calm side

of the island. Mark leads the way with the teenagers, Sonia, Aidan, and Ivy. To get to the leeward cove,
they walk in single file. The path is flanked by wooden
posts painted with creosote. At the beach, the teenagers settle on volcanic rocks that ring the protected bay.
Sonia and Ivy spread their towels on hardened lava,
flat and smooth. When they lie back, their breasts fall
to their sides, straining against the thin bikini tops, the
bright flash of a navel-ring on Ivy's stomach. Aidan
is looking at Ivy from under lowered lashes. Laura remembers the teenage dance, the game of limbs tangled
underwater. Aidan opens his tackle box and iridescent
lures tumble out. As he works, he glances at Ivy, who is
lying with a thin arm thrown over her eyes, exposing
childlike ribs. He baits the rod, the line arcing in a sil-
ver flash over the water.

Laura is ashamed of her swollen stomach, her
veiny thighs. Her leaky body feels old and sad as she
settles on the beach, panting slightly and breathing
through her mouth. Like an old dog. She sits on the
folding chair and puts her feet up on the cooler, her
eyes closing in the heat, dozing under the blue sky, her
eyelashes filtering rainbows. Jeannine settles next to
her, gathering her heavy hair up and into a ponytail.
Laura senses her leaning back, turning her face to the
sun. She wants to remind her to wear sunblock, especially on the star-shaped birthmark that always burns.
Instead she thinks of how she can phrase her words.

"Did Mummy ever brew a tea when you had

cramps?" Laura is drowsy but she takes care with her words.

"Chandelier bush? Once, I think. It tasted terrible. I was sixteen or seventeen," Jeannine says. "We can send the kids to find some. I'll brew some for you tonight; it might help clean you out. Get rid of all that bad blood."

When she opens her eyes, the sun is lower in the sky and Jeannine is drawing a map on a napkin and pointing to the cliff side. Aidan stands watching, opalescent drops of water beading the small of his back.

"Pick as much as you can," Jeannine calls as they leave.

Late afternoon comes, and they have not returned. Laura and Mark mill around the beach, reluctant to leave. But they are old enough to know how to get home. They are probably at the house waiting. When they arrive, the house is silent in the gloom. Sonia's slippers are at the bottom of the stairs, her bikini drying on the line. She, at least, has come back. Just behind the mountain, the new moon is rising, a fingernail sliver of light.

"They didn't go in the boat," says Jeannine, looking out the window. "Even the small skip is here."

On the water, the boat is secure on its mooring.

Mark changes his clothes upstairs. When he comes down, he's packed a small torch and a whistle, passing without touching her. From the jetty she sees where he is going. He is climbing the path to the whale house. Has he forgotten the channel in the side of the cliff, the hidden passage that runs to the heart of the island?

Out of the house, Laura imagines swimming. Under the thin moon, the plankton is glowing, shimmering in the water. Behind their island lies larger Chacachacare, with the decaying buildings of the abandoned leper colony. Its lighthouse, still powered by an ancient cogged wheel, floats on a circular bed of mercury. She's stood here many times, under the copse of trees. She counts thirteen seconds before the beam sweeps the bay. Through the trees, perhaps there is the flicker of a candle throwing shadows on the wall.

In the rainy season, water runs off the land and cascades into the crevice, flattening the wild orchids that cling to the rocks and making the brackish water sweet. The water appears just beyond the trees, the crack in the seamless wall of cliff only visible if you know where to look. Laura unties the skip, sliding the oars into the sea. She manoeuvers the little boat into the stream of water, rowing hard against the current. She rows for ten minutes more, sweating now, and pulls into an alcove with three small steps. Two coconut trees mark the spot and she ties the skip to the first one. The climb is not long but she is winded by the time she reaches the top. The cottage has not changed much. It still stands under the silk cotton tree, its windows shuttered. When she pushes open the door, they don't see her. They are up under the window where the light is green and dim. Aidan is between Ivy's spread honey legs. Ivy sees her first and makes a strangled cry, trying to push Aidan off and cover her breasts. Aidan climbs to his knees and turns to the door. Behind him, she catches a glimpse of Ivy, her pubic hair waxed to a tiny strip above her neat pink slit, the centre moist and slick. Aidan's face is shocked, moonlike in the dim light, his pants around his knees.

Chuck-wit-wit-wee-o, the rufous nightjar calls as she closes the door and runs down the path. Is this what her father saw? When she looks back, they have blown out the candle. Someone else can row the skip home. She is tired. After a few minutes, she veers off the path and lies down on the beaten earth. She does not think of the giant centipedes that live on these rocky islands, hiding under leaf litter. She is too tired to think of them. Far below, she hears the sea as it bucks past the girdled entrance.

"Laura?" Mark is standing over her.

The light from his torch had alerted her but she stayed silent until he rounded the corner and spotted her. She can see he is torn between worry about Aidan and Ivy and his desire to hold onto his anger, which he dares not voice to her.

"They're in the whale house," she says.

In the way of marriages, the unspoken flits yellow between them. She had not wanted Jeannine in the beginning. But that had changed. And it would have been the same for this baby. Baking cakes is not how you throw a baby away. "You think I did it deliberately. You do. But you're wrong," she had said.

In a moment she is on her hands and knees, scrambling to her feet. She could tell him now. If there was ever a moment, it is now. But he has walked away, switching off the torch as he moves back down the path. There is no one else to row the skip home so she rests for a while before going to the boat. The hidden water with its sweetish salt smell rises around her.

At the house, Mark says he will cook dinner. She tells him she will sleep for an hour. They don't touch but the air is no longer muddy between them.

She is still sleeping, deeply and dreamlessly, when Jeannine comes into the bedroom. She wakes Laura with soft strokes along her back.

"Wake up, it's after ten," Jeannine says softly, the room chill with sea air. "This will make you feel better. It will help bring everything down."

Jeannine has brewed a batch of chandelier bush, mamba green in the clear glass. In the dim light, Jeannine's eyes are liquid. She climbs into bed with Laura, pulling the covers over them both. Laura's firstborn is in bed with her. The smell of the tea is the memory of a mother's suspicion, a mother's blame. *I don't understand*, her mother had told Laura. *This baby wants to be born.*

"It will clean out whatever is left," Jeannine says, trailing her fingers over Laura's forehead, making the shushing noises Laura's mother always made when they were sick.

Before midnight, Laura is doubled over with

blinding cramps. On the jetty below, the nightline is ringing. Something big is fighting the hook.

"Laura!" calls Mark.

"What is it? What did you catch?" she answers, matching the excitement in his voice. She knows they will never speak of the baby again.

The memory of the nightline comes back to her from her childhood; the things that would surface from the ocean! Once a four-hundred-pound grouper, once a hammerhead shark with its rows of teeth hidden in its misshapen head, each one rising up out of the black bay, fighting and pulling on the line, the bell ringing and ringing.

By the time she's come down the stairs, they've gutted the shark, an enormous mako with a flat wide head and dead grey skin.

"Come and see."

The rows of tiny sharks are alive, wriggling and squirming in the cavity of their mother. He stands behind her, pulling her back to his chest and rocking her, his head on her chin.

DWIGHT THOMPSON

The Science of Salvation
Jamaica

Youfel Goodman, the spiritual leader of the Montpelier flock of the New Day Revivalists, wakes up
one morning with a divine message. He hurries
to Montpelier Square to stand on the concrete lip of
the old dried-up fountain. He prophesies. People stop
to listen, awed by the spectacle of his countenance,
the timbre of his voice that's like a strange disquieting
wind stirring in their souls.

Tyson is there too. But unlike everyone else listening in mute astonishment, he's weighing the words
carefully, feeling them out for any truth that may lie behind them. Their eyes meet just as Youfel says: ". . . and I
also saw in holy vision, brothers and sisters, that mankind's days are numbered. The future shall be snatched
from the abstraction of his sleep. His dreams shall turn
to dust. His bread shall be his affliction, his water the
wine of wrath. His bed shall become his tomb! Whoso-

ever heareth the voice of God today let him forsake the path of sin. Let him come for his sins to be washed away!"

When he's finished, Youfel steps down and walks through the stunned, murmuring crowd and returns home.

The first stillbirth was brutal. The sky, its womb bursting with rain, bared its teeth and pushed. Dion began drowning in her sleep, dreaming she was engulfed by dead jellyfish on the shore of Fisherman's Cove. She tossed and struggled; she awoke with a start, a nauseating smell like fish glue in her nostrils. Instantly she knew she was in trouble. Thunder pealed above her head and she felt it move inside her. Groaning, she held her stomach and stumbled to the floor, crawling to the bathroom. Writhing in pain against the toilet, she pushed and pushed between clenched teeth till the bloody foetus divorced her body. When she looked at it, it did seem like a mass of jellyfish. Then she passed out. She awoke in the hospital.

The second stillbirth occurred two years later. The village midwife delivered the baby, but she was strangled by the umbilical cord. Dion, aged twenty, marvelled at how peaceful she looked, her body blue like blue soap, the fresh beautiful colour of innocent death, she thought, and was reluctant to part with her. The midwife, a cynical crone who dealt in witchcraft, told her to break the soft anklebones or scar the eyelids, so the baby wouldn't find her way back to her body. It was the first child returned to mock her with death. But Dion refused. She wrapped the umbilical cord in banana leaves and burnt it, as a token of the covenant between her and God to bless her womb, like Hannah praying to Yahweh.

Her miracle came. Towana was born a year later, healthy, beautiful, and noisy. And though the old woman warned her not to be too happy (since death always came in threes), the child blossomed beautifully and was a true source of happiness to her and Youfel.

That had happened eighteen years ago. On the day she lost the first baby, Tyson was sentenced to twenty-two years in prison; now he was out. She'd also had her dream of dead jellyfish again, except that this time Tyson was in the dream, standing above her with his hand on her head (as if about to perform some perverse baptism), but she can't tell whether he's pulling her up to safety or pushing her down to drown. She can't shake the feeling that he would somehow find his way back into their lives, that the past would catch up with them. At a time like this! When she has a child to look out for. It's something not even the magnanimity of her faith can accommodate. The thought of it makes her physically sick.

She didn't have to wait long for her fears to be realized.

Three days after Youfel's sermon, as Dion and Towana return home from Women's Fellowship, they see him, standing outside the shop. Towana points, "Mama, is him name Tyson?"

Dion jerks her arm, "Hush! How many times I must tell you not to point at stranger." Towana nods, feeling her mother's fingernails bite into her flesh, feeling her hand trembling.

"Dion, is not church you coming from? Why you acting so cross? You walk out de little blessin' already."

Tyson braces up off the wall, blowing smoke coolly through his thin dark lips, still looking as lean as when he left for prison. For a time, while still a teenager, after returning home from reformatory school, he was known as the Angel of Death, famed throughout Montego Bay for his maturity, moral code (he never killed civilians, only gang members and other criminals), and strange principles. It's said he allowed his victims to make themselves right with God before killing them, to offer a final prayer or recite scripture, while he watched impassively.

When Dion and Towana are standing close enough he tosses the cigarette stub and smiles; but his eyes are alert and unsmiling, and though it's obvious he's just had a haircut it adds no freshness to his face, which has a blank immobility.

"What a way you daughter big. She looks like Youfel. What's your name, pretty girl?"

Towana ducks behind her mother.

Dion takes a deep breath. "Excuse us." She hurries past him into the shop.

Tyson walks unhurriedly down the steps. "I'll be seeing you again, Dion. Don't worry, we have plenty time to catch up."

When they enter the shop Youfel sees the irritation on Dion's face. Trying to divert her anger, he asks, "Dion, you see the credit book?"

She ignores the question. "I don't want him idling round this shop, you hear me, Youfel? I don't want him within an inch of my child!"

Youfel finds the book. "Dion, the man did his time. Besides, what he ever did to *you?* Why you hate him so much?"

Then Dion realizes what has taken place. That Tyson had come to credit the cigarettes. "Youfel, you must be out of your blasted mind!"

"Dion," Youfel speaks slowly, groping for the right words, "this is a place of business, and I'm an impartial businessman."

Dion is too angry to respond. She storms through the shop's back door, cursing under her breath.

From the radio into the shop's counter, Franklin Knight can be heard putting in his two cents into the ongoing debate over whether persons convicted of capital murder should hang: *"Folks in radioland, listen . . . a growing section of this society has in effect declared war on the society. We may say we can defeat them by killing them, but the fact is we keep reproducing the conditions which create these people who reject society."*

That night, in bed, the world sits on her chest. But

Dion decides that if Tyson is her burden, the reason the sky is falling, she will endure. After all, He never gives us more than we can bear.

Three months pass. Dion sticks to her promise. Whenever Tyson comes to the shop she serves him accordingly. If he requests credit she clears it with Youfel and writes his name in the book. But the sensation of vague fear never leaves her, is always rekindled by his presence.

And he's coming more often now. Soon she catches him and Youfel laughing with the ease of old friends, as if they're still bandmates in the Montego Bay Band. Both boys were drummers, marching up front; she a few rows back, blowing the bugle. That was before Tyson, then aged ten, went to COPS, the boys' home for troubled youngsters, for stabbing Desmond, his grandfather, in his sleep. Just weeks before, Desmond had burnt the boy's back with a clothes iron. Dion watched while they took him away. Tyson cried, not for himself but for his mother, an epileptic whom Desmond often flogged in public. Tyson begged her to leave the house, to move into the women's shelter in the city.

There were other rumours about why Tyson hated Desmond so much: that Desmond had abused him in unspeakable ways. It was also rumoured that Tyson was the product of an incestuous relationship between father and daughter. Dion once asked Youfel about this, but the question only provoked gloomy silence. Dion wonders, too, if it's guilt over not having been able to help Tyson that had prompted Youfel to dedicate his life to saving others. Sometimes she imagines the sky had crashed loudly on Tyson, without warning, before he was strong enough to raise his voice in protest.

Tyson returned home after six years to find fraternity in the Fire-Clappers Crew, Montego Bay's most notorious gang. The next time Desmond tried to have his way with him, Tyson didn't hesitate. One morning the residents woke up to the fetid smell of burnt flesh. They gathered in the street, the women still in night-clothes and curlers, their mouths and noses covered. Desmond had been ringed with tires, doused with petrol, and set ablaze.

The police surmised the significance of what had happened—that the murder marked Tyson's initiation into the gang.

He, along with two other gang members, was convicted of the crime. He was tried as an adult at seventeen but saved from execution because the judge considered his troubled past. He was sentenced to twenty-two years with the possibility of parole, and released after eighteen. During his time in lockup, his mother, with no one to look after her, had suffered an epileptic fit and accidentally drowned.

Tyson took this hard.

Now, Dion waits for Tyson to leave the shop before approaching. "What a way you and him tight," she says mockingly.

Youfel ignores her. When he walks off to serve another customer she examines the entry. She waits until the woman leaves. "Forty dollars! For everyt'ing I jus see him walk out with him, only pay forty dollars. An' already owe us over four hundred from other bills! Youfel, you fraid of him or what? You know him not working. How you expect him to pay us? Fine businessman you are! Why you don't just give him the damn shop. At this rate we soon live on the street!"

Youfel dusts the flour from his hands on his apron.

Dion is fuming. "Leave heathen to their own destruction: that's what I say! That is one soul past saving."

Youfel responds evenly, "I have the power to judge no man, or condemn him. Nor do you."

Dion measures him with a scornful look. "It's a pity your piety can't turn stone to bread. Don't forget you have a family to feed! We not running charity."

On the radio a man is giving Franklin Knight an earful and whipping himself into oratorical frenzy: "*Don't hang them? . . . You want us to spend $700,000,000 instead to feed them at the Iron Bar Hotel; feed them for life! They want television, three meals a day, and if you don't let dem wife in to bring dem food, dem strike.*"

Franklin Knight chuckles: "*Caller, you say the country must act to protect the best interest of its citizens. I agree, but aren't we all citizens of this country, free or detained? Think that over and hold the line, we have to break for the twelve o'clock news . . . The noonday news is brought to you by Cremo. Build a better body with Cremo Milk. A delicious snack now in a handy one-pint pack. Have a good Cremo day today."*

Eight months after Tyson's release, Bussy, another gang member, who'd been convicted with Tyson for Desmond's murder, is released from prison. He challenges Tyson, claiming Tyson is too compromised to be a part of the gang on account of his alleged homosexuality in prison. The gang members take sides. Tyson and his cronies retreat into hiding, strategizing their next move. The atmosphere in the community is tense. People start closing their doors as soon as the sun falls out of the sky.

One Wednesday night, as Dion and some church members are returning home from service, a gunshot rings out close by.

People scream and scramble in all directions. Dion grabs Towana and hoists her over a nearby barbwire fence, then jumps over into the yard; the sharp twisted metal draws her blood. They lie flat in the cold prickly grass, behind a thick hedge. Rapid footfalls approach. Dion's heart is in her throat; Towana's teeth start chattering. Dion closes her eyes and prays fiercely, burying the girl's head in her bosom. When she opens them she sees Marlow and Randy, a few metres ahead, scaling the fence, both of them toting guns. Tyson follows them, jogging in his calm, unhurried way. For a moment he stops, as if about to look back, Dion cringes, then he melts into the shadows by the corner of the house.

Out in the street they cry murder. People mill around the body of Beetle, a boy barely fifteen who was one of Bussy's soldiers. But when the police show up everyone closes their doors. No one saw anything; no one knows anything. Silence is golden.

That night Dion lies awake in bed. She looks over at Youfel staring restlessly at the ceiling, upset with himself for not having accompanied them to temple that night, since he'd been too tired after closing the shop. And though they don't know it, both of them ponder the same thing: their own failures of faith. Youfel is frustrated since no matter how much he reaches out to Tyson he runs into a brick wall; it's hard to read him, hard to make a breakthrough; he refuses Bible study and religious pamphlets; Youfel can't get him to pray with him much less attend church. Youfel wonders if Dion is right, if some people really are beyond saving (and in his heart of hearts, though he'd scarcely admit it to himself, he reaches the conclusion that she must be). Dion wonders about her rekindled uncertainties, about the feeling of moving blindly in the dark, in a cold indifferent place, feeling abandoned by God when she needs Him most. When finally she falls asleep, she dreams. She is cloaked in black, marching in a funeral procession; but when she pushes past everyone to see who's inside the coffin, it's empty; and when she scrutinizes the mourners she realizes they're faceless. She wakes up with a heavy feeling of fear tightening inside her bones, slowly crushing her spirit. The walls are closing in.

On the six a.m. radio news a female reporter says: *"The police have enforced a curfew in the Montego Bay community of Montpelier, following last night's shooting death of Anthony Powell, a.k.a. Beetle, a teenager affiliated with the local Fire-Clappers Crew. The killing is allegedly linked to a gang feud in the area. Persons with information about the incident are being urged to contact the Montpelier Police . . ."*

She hadn't told Youfel what she'd witnessed, and had sworn Towana to secrecy. But Dion decides to act, to break the silence, refusing to surrender to fear or cowardice. Something must be done. She shouldn't wait for God to save her. After all, isn't He waiting for us to take the initiative sometimes? Isn't faith without works dead? She will follow her instinct to protect her family. She will rid Tyson from their lives once and for all.

Just as he passes the temple, heading to the shop, Tyson gets the call. It's his informant at the police station. Someone just named him as being involved in the killing of the teenage boy. He listens with a tight expression, then hangs up, leaning against a lamppost to collect himself. Pulling the cap down over his face, he moves toward the boy catching water at the standpipe. He takes the bucket from him and fills it. Then gives him the cell phone as a gift, for being so helpful. The boy can hardly believe his luck; he thanks Tyson shyly and runs off to boast to his friends. The temple is filling its pool for baptismal service that weekend and the children are helping the deaconesses on duty. Tyson enters the church; as he empties the bucket in the pool, the women recognize him. The head deaconess, a heavyset, cheerful woman who used to scold him and Youfel as boys for cutting school, steps forward. "Tyson, you coming to service this weekend?"

He doesn't answer, but stares curiously into the artificial shimmer of the filling pool, the water light green and frothy with added chlorine. "Sister, you should buy a hose. What you people collecting offerings for?" He takes the money from his pocket, the seven hundred dollars he'd intended to pay Youfel for his debts, and puts it into the woman's hand, curling her fingers around it. Then he slips out the back door, cutting through yards and open lots until he comes out at the bridge over the river on the east side of the community. For a moment he stands with his hands on his hips, catching his breath, looking wildly around as if he doesn't know where he is, as if he's being pursued by phantoms; he smashes the rail with his fist and swears, then sits on the ground and grips his head in his hands. "It has to be done," he whispers, "it has to be done."

From a car stereo, Franklin Knight's disembodied voice floats above the turbulent hiss of water rushing over stones and pebbles in the riverbed below: "*Sometimes you have to hit rock bottom before you realize the Lord is the Rock at the bottom. Isn't that a comforting thought? Sent to me by one of my longtime listeners, Ms. Merle up*

*in Walkerswood. How the pimento crop coming in this
year, Ms. Merle? Walk good in Walkerswood. I'm Franklin
Knight and this has been* Frankly Speaking. *Until tomorrow, take good care of you and yours."*

When Tyson kicks in their back door that night Dion
feels cheated. Her helplessness has a cruel sense of irony.
For while she'd felt justified in acting to save her family; she now feels reproached, especially when she sees
the fear in Towana's eyes, knowing she's damned the
very life she'd sworn to protect.

Marlow and Randy stand behind Tyson, their
weapons drawn. Youfel kneels at the foot of the bed
between the men and his family. Marlow's eyes follow
the stream of urine glistening down Towana's trembling thigh. Dion holds the child tight, closing her eyes
automatically to pray. But her mouth won't move. Her
mind won't tick. And in the vacuum of her paralysis
she feels like renouncing the very name of God with
the angry bewilderment of her failing flesh.

Gunfire barks in the distance.

"Dion, I told you I'd see you again."

She looks at him steadily. "Do your worst, Tyson.
I'm not afraid to die. To cling to life is to cling to death."

Tyson smiles and applauds. "Well said . . . What a
way you get brave. That's why you sell me out to police
today, eh? Little Miss Neighborhood Watch. But don't
worry, Tyson never put him gun on no civilian, everybody know that. Anybody die by my hands deserve it.

There'll be no scripture reading or praying tonight. Tonight I'm the Angel of Mercy." He glares at Youfel. "Stand up, preacher! What you doing on your knees before a sinner?" He drags Youfel to his feet.

"Daddy!" Towana lunges across the bed at her father but Dion pulls her back. The child weeps in her mother's embrace.

"Is all right, baby," Tyson says, shoving Youfel forward. "I jus go talk to Daddy."

Youfel walks slowly but stops in the doorway. "Tyson, please. Don't let them rape—"

But Tyson puts his finger to Youfel's lips. Then they're out the door.

Outside the night breeze plays cool over Youfel's skin. As he walks ahead of Tyson down the stony path, a gun to his back, he listens keenly for the voices of his family but only hears sporadic gunfire and the murmur of his neighbour's radio filtering through the sheets of zinc fencing: *Here now is a special item of news: Less than two hours ago, gunmen firebombed sections of the Montpelier Police Station. Police and soldiers are still scrambling to put out the blaze while warding off armed and brazen criminals, who are leading a sustained attack on the security forces and presently running amok in sections of the small community. The surge of violence is in response to the recent curfew in the area following the slaying of teenager Anthony 'Beetle' Powell. So far a policeman has reportedly sustained a gunshot injury. His condition is unknown.*

Youfel wills himself to pray, but like Dion the words won't come. It's as if his faith has flown.

They come out on the sparsely populated side of the community, walking down the hillside that lets out along the shoreline of Fisherman's Cove, the sand and beach purplish-black in the distance. As they walk, Youfel reflects on the trajectory of his life: from chosen prophet to defenceless victim, at the mercy of a man he'd once called friend, soon, very likely, to be killed.

They descend the hill, are on the beach, on the dark side of the mountain where early-morning mist always sits as if sleeping.

Meanwhile, a special team of soldiers and police, acting on intelligence, has just surrounded Youfel's house.

Youfel doesn't know why but he kicks off his sandals; the black sand is cool and compact under his feet. The two men walk side by side. Youfel glances at Tyson. His long thin face is calm, betrays no emotion. As if responding to his stare, Tyson says, "Youfel, that day by the square, you said that if you believe, your faith will make you whole."

Youfel is momentarily baffled, then realizes Tyson's referring to his testimony in the square that morning after his vision. "Yes . . ."

"An' you said the man who goes down in the watery grave of baptism comes out a new man, free from the shackles of the past."

"Yes, but—"

Tyson stops and points at the foaming sea. "Here is water, what is stopping me from being baptized?"

Youfel is thrown. "But . . . when did you see the light?"

"Little by little, day by day. When you give a listening ear at the shop. When you trust me enough to credit me your goods and expect payment."

Youfel's confusion slowly gives way to realization, then anger. "So why the abduction? Why the guns?"

"It was the only way to get you down here. This is where I must be baptized, in the same sea that take my mother's life. My new life must begin where hers ended. Don't worry bout your family, no harm coming to them. Things go get ugly tonight. You hear the gunshots. The turf war start. Later on they will loot an' rape; innocent people will suffer. The boys have instructions to take your family to a safe house until things cool off. Two more will come an' watch the shop. Just to be on the safe side. You have my word."

Youfel is still too stunned to speak.

"I am the man with the price on my head," Tyson continues. "The police and half the Fire-Clappers hunting me. I must leave this place tonight. But I must break with the past. I'm not asking for a clear conscience, just an opportunity to start over." He looks pleadingly at Youfel. "I realize no matter how far I run I can't run from myself. But this is a start . . . this is the way to freedom . . . else I will die inside long before they catch up with me. You must baptize me, Youfel . . . you must save me."

An exchange of gunfire roars above the hill.

But Youfel barely registers the sound, so engrossed is he in the mystery—no, the science—of salvation unfolding before his eyes. He feels a sudden ripple of rage, which dissolves into shame. He shakes his head, his eyes squeezed shut. "No, no. It is *you* who have saved *me* from self-doubt, and saved my family from potential harm. It is you who have rescued my faith, by showing me what true faith is . . ."

In the aftermath of the shootout, Marlow and Randy lie dead in the yard. The lawmen had surprised them as they left the house; they'd been quickly cut down.

Dion had run back inside the house and quickly gone to the floor in the crossfire, her body shielding Towana's. Now she eases up slowly and cautiously, hearing the reassuring sound of the policemen's boots ascending the back steps. She stares in disbelief. The child is covered in blood, her face frozen, as she sucks down what's possibly her final breath; her wide-mouthed gaze seems to make the accusation: *Mama, why didn't you protect me?* Dion opens her mouth to scream but the burning sensation spreads inside her chest, nausea rises in her throat, she coughs and warm fluid fills her mouth. She realizes the blood is in fact hers and that it's flowing quickly. She's suddenly weak. Then everything is blackness.

Tyson tosses the gun on the sand. He sheds his shirt,

dropping it by his feet. Youfel sees the scar on his back, where Desmond had pressed the hot iron; in the moonlight it comes alive, a twisting serpent burrowing deeper into his flesh. Tyson enters the water, kneeling so that it reaches his waist, his head bowed, his hands clasped.

Youfel hears the rumble of the engine and looks up to see the squad car cresting the hill. He hurries to Tyson and lifts him by the shoulders, making the sign of the cross and kissing the man's forehead. Tyson weeps.

"Rise, my son," Youfel says, "your faith has already made you whole. Now it's time to run."

Moments later, as he stands on the shore, reflecting on the miracle that had been wrought, a stubborn soul finally won, a policeman approaches Youfel with heavy footsteps and a solemn face. Maybe he's coming to arrest him. But Youfel's heart is light. After all, he thinks, what does this man know about the sweetness of life?

KEVIN BALDEOSINGH

Cheque Mate
Trinidad & Tobago

The bank teller looked like a sensible woman. She wore spectacles with sensible black wire frames; her black hair was tied back in a sensible bun unstreaked by red or blonde highlights; even her stocky figure in her grey bank uniform looked sensible. But she wasn't making any sense.

Sukiya heard the words like a foreign language as the teller repeated her question: "Ms. Chansing? Do you want the thirty million dollars deposited in your savings account or would you prefer to open a US dollar account?"

Sukiya glanced around the banking hall. She had deliberately not come to the branch where she had her savings account, because the staff there would be too familiar with her business. She was in the special queue for customers who held platinum credit cards. There were just two people behind her, but they were not close enough to hear what the teller was saying. The other queue, for ordinary customers, had twenty-two people standing between the velvet ropes which hung like sleeping snakes between stainless steel stanchions. At the head of that line, a man in a green khaki shirt and black trousers stood with his brown leather shoes just touching red tape on the polished marble floor. An orange arrow on the bank counter's electronic strip lit up and the man moved toward a wicket on the far side of the counter. Twenty-one people in the line now, nine at the counter, four in the line for commercial transactions, and three in the special line. A total of thirty-seven customers. Sukiya's tally was automatic and effortless. She counted everything, which was why the teller standing in front of her was making no sense at all.

Was it some kind of joke? Sukiya looked at the woman, who was gazing expectantly back at her. She didn't seem to be joking, but if she was, Sukiya would write a formal complaint to the manager. Perhaps she should have been talking to the manager in the first place. But, from the day she was appointed corporate secretary of the company and got a tenfold salary raise, Sukiya had decided that she would not deal with any bank managers, even though she was now among the country's one percent of highest income earners. Her official tax-deductible salary was standard for top executives: the fifty thousand dollars went automat-ically into her savings account on the twenty-eighth day of every month. But that money didn't show her real income, which was how Randall had advised her to arrange her finances. Sukiya only used that savings account to pay the mortgage on her two-bedroom apartment on the island and related monthly bills, mainly utilities. The rest of the money just accumulated. The company paid for gas and servicing of her SUV, an Audi Q7; she ate out for most meals, including breakfast, which she usually had at the hotel across the road from the company's headquarters at seven every morning except Sunday; and for every other expense, even hairstyling and shoes, she used the company credit card.

Her savings account now had just over seven million dollars in it. She had become the company's corporate secretary six years ago, but had been working there for fifteen years. In the first decade, when she had just been one of several in-house lawyers, her savings had never crossed ten thousand dollars. Now she deposited five times that amount every month in that same account, which she had opened when she was eighteen years old and was working as a store clerk. This was the reason why, after her promotion, Sukiya had decided never to deal personally with the bank manager, as most customers in her new income bracket did. A bank manager might wonder how a fifty-thousand-a-month salary became seven million dollars in savings within six years, and he would know enough to make some educated guesses. An ordinary teller, on the other hand, would know little about how rich people conducted their business. She would see Sukiya's salary, and record the cheques that she came in with every few months to deposit, but at most the teller would just be envious that this woman was earning hundreds of times more money than she made as a bank clerk.

Except, now, Sukiya was facing one of those very tellers and feeling a flutter in her stomach. She said, "What you mean—" then stopped. She took a breath to make sure her voice was steady and, making sure to pronounce each word properly, said, "I don't understand what you mean. That cheque is for five million dollars."

The teller nodded. "Yes, Ms. Chansing. It's for five million dollars US. If you're depositing the cheque in your savings account, I just have to contact our treasury department to get exchange-rate approval, but it should be about 30,242,000 Trinidad and Tobago dollars." She gestured with the cheque, and Sukiya almost flinched. "Or would you like to open a US dollar account?"

The teller, in her sensible bank uniform with her sensible hairstyle, began to recite the benefits of a US account for that sum of money, but Sukiya, aghast at her own carelessness, barely heard her. A US dollar cheque. She wouldn't have made such a mistake sixteen years ago when she was just a twenty-five-year-old attorney fresh out of law school. She wouldn't have made it seven years ago, when she finally completed her degree in accounting, the same year her father had died from kidney failure at San Fernando General Hospital where there were only two dialysis machines. He had not known that Sukiya was studying accounts or that she had been making enough money to put him in a private clinic or even, if she'd wanted, send him to Pakistan for a new kidney. Now, she had actually tossed a multimillion-dollar cheque into her desk drawer without reading the figure properly. It had been her responsibility to move vast sums through various channels when the oil and gas boom started and the money began flowing into the company. It wasn't the kind of mistake she'd ever made before.

"Gimme the cheque," Sukiya told the teller. The woman's eyes widened a little. Had her tone been too abrupt? "Please," she added.

The teller slid the cheque across the counter. Sukiya picked it up, the serrated edge familiar against her fingertips, and scanned the black ink stamped irrefutably into the heavy paper: five million dollars US, made out in her name, signed *Randall A. Credo* with the firm downstroke on the *R* and the large loop on the *C*, countersigned by herself in her neat and precise handwriting. She hadn't even looked when she'd signed it, partly because the cheque had been part of a rushed session one week ago in which she had signed off forty-seven different documents with Randall. But that was no excuse. She had made a mistake, and she never made mistakes.

There was just one person in the line behind Sukiya now, thirty-three people in the line for ordinary bank accounts, six in the commercial queue. Forty customers, not including herself. None of the women was as well-dressed as Sukiya, and she had seen some of them glancing at her Burberry skirt and Dolce blouse and Manolo Blahnik pumps. Sukiya had intended to go back to the office after finishing her business in the bank, but now she was worried. It was twelve minutes until noon, and then there would be more customers and the banking hall would be nearly full because the ordinary accounts line would stretch from counter to door. She wanted to be out of the bank before that happened.

But she couldn't deposit the five million—or, rather, the $30,242,000—into her local account. It wasn't just because all her US cheques went to the Cayman Islands account, which was the money she used to invest and to pay the mortgage on her London flat. Randall had inherited his company long before electronic banking was standard, and he had watched too many movies where unrealistically cunning criminals cleaned out businessmen's offshore bank accounts by hacking into them. So he preferred to do these payments in paper; but Sukiya didn't know why Randall had given her this five million dollars. She couldn't deposit it until she had spoken to him. But would the teller get suspicious if she took the cheque back?

She looked at the woman again. The frames of her spectacles were inexpensive. She wore a wedding ring, but the diamond was small and standard-cut. The skin of her face was very smooth, though she wasn't unusually pretty. The other seven cheques Sukiya had given her were heaped in a little stack; Sukiya would have laid them out so she could scan all the details in one glance. No, she decided, the woman had no inkling of how finance really worked.

"You could tell me . . ." Sukiya paused, drawing another breath. "Could you tell me the amounts of those cheques?" The figures ran automatically through her head: 67,000 last September; 129,000 in November; 82,000 in December; 240,000 in January; 400,000 in April; 322,000 in May; and 600,000 in August. She had gotten the five million cheque last Tuesday, which she had assumed was her fee for the contract she had drawn up for Randall to sell the methanol plant. So she had decided that she should go to the bank and deposit all the cheques in the drawer before they added up to real money.

The teller took up the seven cheques and flipped through them top to bottom as she read out the dates and totals. Sukiya wanted those few moments to think, and to make sure that she hadn't, somehow, made another mistake. But the sums the teller called out matched the numbers in Sukiya's head. The total was $1,840,000. It wasn't much money in the real world— just about $300,000 US, or 215,000 euros, or 180,000 pounds sterling—but Sukiya knew she shouldn't have let it pile up like that. It was just that she hated going to the bank, joining lines of people to deposit pieces of trivial paper, when she usually sat in her office and dealt with real money on the computer.

"Okay," she told the teller, "put those in my account. I go—I will open a US savings account as you advised, but I don't have time now. I could come back later?"

"Of course, Ms. Chansing," the teller said. "We're closing at two today, though."

"I'll come back tomorrow to see about that, then. What time you open . . . do you open?"

"At eight. And you'll need to provide the source of funds, of course."

"Of course," Sukiya said, biting down a pleased smile at this confirmation that the teller had no idea how really rich people conducted their business. She waited patiently while the teller signed off the seven cheques and, after punching the figures into her computer, printed out a deposit slip which she handed to Sukiya.

"I've confirmed the company account and cleared your cheques so you have access to the funds," she said.

"Thank you for your help," Sukiya answered, and left the bank, where she now counted a total of fifty-five customers. As she walked back to the car park, she felt pleased at how she had handled that potentially awkward encounter. People were difficult to read, not like numbers, but she had distracted the teller, took charge of her, and then made her feel that she had done a good job. Sukiya's only criticism of herself was her occasional lapse into the countryside accent of her up-bringing, but even there she had caught herself before the teller could glean where Sukiya was from.

Besides, the teller wasn't in her class now. If Sukiya really had opened a US dollar account for five million, she supposed the teller would get some kind of boost in her performance evaluation, maybe even a promotion. What would that be worth to her? Maybe an extra two thousand dollars a month? A five-thousand-dollar bonus at the end of the year? Sukiya smiled as she pressed the unlock button on her key remote and climbed into the SUV. She could have been like that teller, but she had worked hard and found a way to leave the poverty she had been born into. The teller might even have a life insurance policy with the company; more than one-third of the island's population did. Sukiya pressed her forefinger to the electronic ignition and fastened her seat belt as the engine hummed to life, thinking that, statistically, 33 percent of the customers in the ordinary accounts line had paid for her Audi.

But they had not paid the US five million dollars now sitting in her wallet. That must have come from the Chinese, though Sukiya didn't know why. She settled into the leather seat, the air-conditioning creating an autumnal cocoon against the shimmering tropical heat outside, and pulled out of the crowded car park. She would have to go to her apartment before she headed back to the office. She needed to check her private records before she saw Randall. And she wanted to change her clothes. She had no meetings scheduled today, so she had dressed for style. But, if she was to meet Randall, she wanted to be wearing a more formal outfit. It was, Sukiya had learned long ago, necessary for a woman, even if she had known her boss (and his secrets) for so many years.

She turned onto the road leading out of the city. Her apartment, located in a suburb where the wealthiest 1 percent of the population lived, was a ten-minute drive away, but at peak hours the traffic stretched that time to forty minutes or even an hour. Randall would be furious if her mistake had exposed him to any legal investigation, or even just public embarrassment, and a furious Randall Credo frightened even his toughest top executives. But there was little chance of public embarrassment: all the politicians wanted the company's money for campaign funding, their pet projects, and, of course, their personal bank accounts. The company also had shares in every major media house on the island, so no reporter would be looking for a scandal there, and even if one did, no editor would let it be published for fear of a backlash from the advertising department or, worse, their board of directors.

She wondered if Randall himself had made an error by giving her this cheque. Perhaps, in that exercise which had taken them the entire morning, he had confused one payment with another. Had he seemed distracted? She didn't think so. He had worked with his usual fierce concentration, discussing the various points of each transaction succinctly and quickly, and the only interruption in their intense flow was trivial, when his pen had run out of ink as he was signing documents and he had borrowed her eighteen-carat Tibaldi rollerball—and, Sukiya only now realised, had forgotten to give it back. And the thought popped automatically into her head, as inevitable as the logic of two plus two equals four: should she just *not* mention the cheque to Randall and deposit it into her Cayman account? Sukiya played with this possibility for several minutes as she waited for the traffic light to change. Even for her, US five million was a substantial sum. She could use the money to renovate her London flat; or she could buy the adjacent unit in her Miami condominium and convert the place into a three-bedroom space; or, for just fourteen million TT dollars, she could buy a six-bedroom house with a swimming pool and gazebo.

As the lights turned green and Sukiya pulled out into the three-lane main road out of the city, she decided against depositing the cheque without consulting Randall. Her London and Miami properties were good investments, and she would get her mother's modest three-bedroom flat when she died. Besides, wealthy as he was, even Randall didn't throw around cheques for that amount; and she, as corporate secretary and his private accountant, would have known about such a sum too. He didn't have her foolproof mind for calculations, but he could look at a row of numbers in an income statement, or a balance sheet, or an equity statement, and instantly know what they meant. He didn't need to calculate: he just knew intuitively if the figures were off, if they concealed something, or what they meant as a transaction. Sukiya respected this ability, although she had rejected her mathematical gift in favour of law, because lawyers earned more than accountants and because her father had been an accounts clerk who, when Sukiya at seventeen years had won the national scholarship that provided the money for her to go to university, had celebrated by getting even drunker and beating her mother more viciously than usual.

But Randall, whose father had been one of the country's leading businessmen, had a similar ability for law as for accounts. Sukiya as corporate secretary drew up contracts, studied conveyances, and wrote legal opinions, and she knew all the requirements for such documents. Randall could read the documents and see the potential loopholes. When she had first been promoted, Sukiya thought Randall had hired her to close such loopholes; instead, she got her largest cheques for creating them. The sale of the methanol company to the Chinese government had been a standard contract, however, and that was the only task she had done for which she could be paid a large sum. But not US five million, even with the bribe which the Chinese considered protocol in such deals.

Sukiya drummed her fingers impatiently on the steering wheel. It was now the lunch hour and the traf-

fic had already slowed to a crawl, as those office work-
ers with vehicles and assigned parking spaces headed
like so many beetles to restaurants outside the city to
have lunch. The traffic was worse these days because
of the skyscrapers being built on the waterfront property of the island's main harbour: sleek glass-and-
steel towers that, even before completion, glowed
with pastel-coloured liner lights during the night.
These buildings were the prime minister's pet project,
and he was using the new inflow of oil and gas dollars to change the city's skyline to a facade of Miami's.
Randall was a major campaign contributor, so the company had gotten several contracts for the construction,
and Sukiya usually didn't mind the traffic since she had
bought her Q7. She liked the vehicle's high vantage
point, and the fact that there were very few Audi SUVs
on the road, and the quietness of the engine. But, most
of all, Sukiya liked that no one could see her through
the windows which were tinted far darker than the
legal limit (the traffic police would know they would be
wasting their time charging anyone who drove a vehicle which cost more than an ordinary person's house).
Today, though, none of these thoughts calmed her. She
needed to find out if any mistake had been made, and
she needed to get to her apartment so she could be fully
prepared when she met Randall.

She took out her iPhone and opened the organ-
iser to check the day's schedule: Randall had meetings
all afternoon at the office, so he would be there. She

had known that. She pressed the home button and said, enunciating each syllable, "Secretary Margaret." When Randall's executive assistant answered her call, Sukiya told her to open a ten-minute slot for her before two o'clock. Margaret asked if one thirty would be convenient and Sukiya said yes. She didn't think it would take longer than that to clarify the matter—and, Sukiya suddenly decided, if there *had* been a mistake which was not her fault, she was sure she could persuade Randall to let her keep the cheque. After all, the sale to the Chinese had taken a lot of work, and had been very profitable—and Randall had been able to pocket a sum of money which made the cheque in Sukiya's purse look like spare change.

This thought stayed in her mind as she entered her apartment twenty minutes later. The traffic had started flowing once she was out of the city. The noon heat had broiled her briefly as she got out of her SUV and walked to the elevator, and she vented a short sigh of pleasure at the chill breeze of her apartment's air-conditioning when she opened the door. She sat down on her cream leather sofa and pushed off her shoes. The maid had already come and gone and the apartment had its usual pristine unlived-in look. The white rugs were spotless, the stone countertop and steel-and-glass dining table gleamed, and the sofa set shone with leather polish. Getting up with a slight grunt, Sukiya selected a key from her key ring and unlocked her study. The maids were never allowed in there, even when she was present. Apart from her confidential work documents, they might wonder about the four steel eyelets embedded in the wall, or seen the leather toys she kept in the trunk under the iron-framed cot.

The room also had two filing cabinets and a computer desk with an ergonomic office chair. Cardboard folders and plastic binders were piled everywhere, and there was dust on the computer keyboard. Sukiya sat in the chair and pulled open a desk drawer. There were ten cheques inside, which she laid out neatly on the desktop. She took the one out of her wallet and placed it at the centre of the square of cheques. She had gotten these cheques over a three month period. In all, they totalled US twelve million dollars. It was Randall's fault that she had almost made the mistake with this new one. He insisted on paying for her extra duties involving foreign firms with US cheques. So, every two months, Sukiya had to fly from Trinidad to Grand Cayman to deposit them into her account there. But then she had also started hoarding the TT-dollar cheques, which were paid on the side for tasks involving local transactions. Sukiya found it onerous to deposit those cheques regularly, and months would drag on before she reached the local bank. She realised that there was an element of vanity in this: she took pleasure in the fact that she, a poor girl from Penal, was now so prosperous that she could let millions of dollars accumulate in a desk drawer without any need for the money.

But she kept both her US and TT cheques in the same drawer, and that was how the mix-up occurred. Why should she have thought a five-million-dollar cheque was in US dollars? And why had Randall given her such a huge fee?

Sukiya booted up the desktop computer. She was not as paranoid as Randall, but this computer, on which she kept her confidential records, had no Internet access. For that she used her laptop, netbook, and iPhone. When the screen came on, she put in her password, then opened a folder with another password, and then the spreadsheets in the folder. First she checked her accounts over the past year, then she compared her recent transactions with the cheques laid out in front her. Everything matched, except this five million. Once again, she wondered if she should just keep quiet and fly out to the Caymans next week. She had been thinking about getting a new place for some months now. The apartment had seemed luxurious when she first bought it, three months into her new post. But now she found it a little cramped, especially this room which served as her study-cum-playroom, and which ended up being used more for play than for study. It seemed that there were always rich and powerful men who liked to be powerless, if only for a night. Sukiya glanced at the far wall: if she moved, she would have to take out the steel eyelets from the wall. She had placed the top ones a little too low, for many of the men were above average in height and she liked their arms fully stretched; she would have to remedy that if and when she bought a new place.

Sukiya shook her head, annoyed at getting ahead of herself. She had to concentrate. She went over the spreadsheets again, and then a third time, making sure that her records were accurate and, more importantly, that the records which were not supposed to be accurate were not accurate in the right way. Everything was in order, as she had expected. She didn't make mistakes.

Next she examined the US cheques laid out on the desktop. The sums were right, the dates correct, every one signed by Randall and countersigned by herself. So now the only thing to do was to take the cheque to Randall and hear his explanation. It would probably turn out to be something quite simple, such as a surprise bonus. True, Randall was not the kind of man to spring such surprises, and Sukiya didn't think he would expect anything in return. He had made his pass even before her promotion, been rebuffed, and had still given her the post. But she thought she would nonetheless dress with special care for her meeting with him.

She rose and went to the master bedroom, pulling off her blouse and unhooking her skirt. She tossed the clothes on her queen-sized four-poster bed, and slid open the mirrored door of her closet. Sukiya knew what she would wear: her royal-blue Armani skirt suit. She pulled out the suit along with a pink camisole and closed the closet door, then examined herself in the mirror: her body was slim even though she didn't really exercise, and the slackness of her tummy was not noticeable when she was dressed. She didn't like her skin, which was dry and blemished with occasional dark spots; but Sukiya never let men see her naked in bright light, even when she wore her special outfits. She pulled the camisole over her head, then stepped into the skirt, zipping up the waist which fit with snug comfort, and then put on the jacket. She looked in the mirror again. The jacket fit perfectly, the camisole's pink lace peeping out from the top button. She didn't think Randall really noticed her appearance anymore, but he was a man and Sukiya wanted every advantage if the meeting turned into a negotiation.

She went back to the study and took an empty manila envelope from the filing cabinet, wondering if she should carry all the cheques or just the new one which had disrupted her day. And then, as she stood over the desk frowning, Sukiya saw what was wrong with them. She heard her breath gasp from her throat, as though from someone else. She closed her eyes for several seconds, and then looked down again at the rectangles of paper neatly arranged on her desk. She still saw what she had seen, like the hidden shape in a collection of dots. There was no mistake, which meant that Randall A. Credo was either clinically insane or even more cunning than she had thought.

Sukiya felt the tension in her thighs and knees, and realised that she was trying to stop her legs from buckling. She carefully rolled the office chair back and sat down. She ran light, unsteady fingers over the cheques. Options clicked through her mind, like the various clauses she put into contracts to achieve certain ends or to prevent the other party from achieving certain ends. But she knew that there were really only two options: confront Randall or run away. She could run away: she had more than enough money. But she'd had more than enough money for several years now. To run away would mean she could no longer be a player in the world's most important game.

Sukiya stood up. She gathered up all the cheques and put them into the manila envelope. Her hands were steady now. She would go and meet Randall for their one thirty meeting. She only hoped that he was just insane.

The trip back into the capital city took just ten minutes. Sukiya used that time to plan her strategy. She parked in her space in the company car park. It was one fifteen. She sat in her Q7. She didn't want to go to Randall's office and be kept waiting because she was early. That would put her in a position of weakness. Nor did she want to arrive late, for Randall insisted on punctuality. She waited until 1:25, then took the elevator to the top floor, walking into Randall's outer office at exactly 1:29. The secretary, Margaret, was at her desk, as always. Sukiya raised her eyebrows at Randall's door.

Margaret nodded and said, "I opened a slot as you requested. He's expecting you." Margaret was a middle-aged woman with a little-girl lilt in her voice.

She always wore low-heeled shoes and straight skirts that reached below her knees. She had been Randall's secretary even before he inherited the company. Despite having no formal skills except typing and shorthand, she now functioned as Randall's executive assistant, and actually had her own secretary to deal with routine duties. Margaret's office was bigger than Sukiya's, but Sukiya put this down to architectural necessity since the office was really Randall's. Yet Margaret was also paid more than most managers in the company's sub-sidiaries, and Sukiya felt this was because the woman knew more about Randall's dealings than anyone else in the company—including Sukiya herself.

She knocked on Randall's door and heard his usual gruff, "Come in." Sukiya entered, holding the manila envelope tightly in her hand.

Randall was sitting behind his oak desk, examining some files. His office was huge, and light and airy, with large rectangular plate-glass windows set deep into the wall. The office contained a small conference table at one end, and had a sofa set in a corner. Randall was dressed, as usual, in a suit which looked one size too small for his stocky frame. He did not smile to greet her—Randall's face was not shaped for smiling, and the best he ever did was a slight stretch of the lips. In its casual brutality, his visage always reminded Sukiya of the unforgiving god-masks of certain Amerindian tribes. He had a wide but tight-lipped mouth, a thick nose, and a hard chin. Only Randall's light-brown eyes would have been attractive, except for his habitually sharp gaze.

"What can I do for you, Sukiya?" Randall never wasted time on small talk, which was a habit that he and Sukiya shared.

She pulled the cheque out of her purse and dropped it on the desk. "I don't know what this is for."

Randall picked it up. His fingers were thick, with black hairs on the backs of the joints. He examined the cheque for several seconds. "I was wondering if you would query this or just deposit it," he said. "When I didn't hear from you for one week, I assumed you'd deposited it."

"What's it for?"

"On the books, it's your fee for the methanol deal."

"And off the books?"

"Off the books, it's your fee for keeping your mouth shut about the methanol deal."

Sukiya folded her arms. "Why do I need to keep my mouth shut, Randall? I drew up a standard contract."

He reached into a drawer and pulled out a plastic-covered folder. "This is a valuation report for the shares. The contract you drew up undervalues those shares by 50 percent."

Sukiya blinked. "I used the share price you told me to use."

Randall opened the folder to the last page, and pointed to a signature at the bottom. "You've gotten into the habit of signing documents without reading them properly, Sukiya."

Sukiya's lips tightened. She understood now. This was why the Chinese had offered such a huge kickback. Randall had offered them the methanol plant at below value, but if anyone found out about the valuation it could be the basis for fraud charges. She said, "Your signature's there too."

Randall shrugged. "I didn't write the contract."

Sukiya opened the flap on the manila envelope. "You've acquired some peculiar signing habits too, Randall." She shook out the cheques and laid them in front of him. Randall looked down at the slips of paper, and then did what Sukiya thought he'd never do: he smiled. His smile was a tight curve of the lips, and he showed no teeth, but there was genuine pleasure in it.

"Finally," he said.

The nervousness Sukiya felt in the bank that morning had merely caused a flutter in her stomach. Now she felt as though her stomach was a cold, tight ball. Her mouth had gone dry. She drew a deep breath and kept her voice steady.

"Your signatures on these cheques don't match. Each one looks different. Only that one," she nodded at the five-million-dollar cheque at the centre, "is written in your normal hand."

Randall's smile became even wider, but his teeth were still covered by his lips. "Actually, it's only *close* to my normal hand. Apparently, someone in this office had access to blank cheques and forged my signature. Even the signature on this cheque, which as you say is quite close to mine, was written with your pen." He pulled out her Tibaldi rollerball from his inside pocket. "It's quite a nice pen."

Sukiya licked her lips. "What are you up to, Randall?"

He gestured to his desk, which was covered with files, reports, and business magazines. "The universe is collapsing, Sukiya, and its masters cannot hold."

Sukiya sucked her teeth; Randall's habit of uttering cryptic statements had always annoyed her, and she was in no mood to decipher. "What does that mean?"

"It means, Sukiya, that this company will be bankrupt within three months."

The shimmer from the giant windows seemed to become stronger, as though the light had begun to vibrate. Sukiya leaned forward, resting the palms of her hands on Randall's desk. "We can't be bankrupt. We're one of the biggest conglomerates in the region."

Now Randall showed his teeth as he laughed, and Sukiya's stomach clenched even tighter. "I think there's going to be a worldwide financial crisis before the year is finished. You might not see that, you don't pay attention to the world. But you've been moving this company's assets around for years. You know our finances better than anyone. You didn't see it coming?"

"I did what you told me to do," she said. "And why have you forged your own signature on your own cheques?"

Randall shrugged. "Just protecting myself. When the storm breaks, I'll be in its eye. The cheques are just one strategy. The managers, the board, yourself—well, let's just say that none of the documents the authorities will come for implicate me."

"You're the boss. You'll be held accountable!" She spoke more vehemently than she had intended.

"I may be held responsible," Randall answered, "but there'll be nothing to hold me *accountable*." He rolled her pen like a propeller between his fingers. "A crucial difference."

And then what Sukiya had never let happen in her whole professional career happened: her eyes grew hot and prickly and tears sprouted onto her cheeks. Randall watched her curiously. "Relax, Sukiya. You may have to go to court, but the police here don't have the technical know-how to make a case for financial transgressions."

Sukiya wiped her wet face with the back of her hand. After a few moments, she said, "If we collapse, that affects every person who has a life insurance policy with us. That means votes. That means the government will hire American forensic auditors, probably even British QCs, to prosecute the case."

Randall nodded. "There is that possibility."

Sukiya leaned forward, her white knuckles pressed into the hard oak of Randall's desk. "I've always been loyal to you—"

Randall cut her off: "You were certainly paid enough to be loyal."

Sukiya breathed deeply, and she saw Randall's eyes shift to her cleavage. "Can't you help me?" she said quietly.

Seconds of silence ticked away. Finally, Randall said, "Come here."

Sukiya hesitated, then went around the desk. Randall turned in his black leather chair to face her. He had stopped smiling. "Kneel," he said. His knees shifted, opening a space between his legs. "Kneel," he said again.

Sukiya licked her lips. She pulled her hair back. Then her iPhone beeped. "Excuse me," she told Randall.

She pulled the phone out of the inside pocket of her Armani jacket, peered at the screen, and pressed some buttons. Randall frowned, and Sukiya held up a forefinger as she put the phone to her ear. Randall's lips thinned to a vicious line. More seconds passed. Finally, she turned back to him. "I know you don't like technology, Randall. But it really is wonderful."

She pressed a button on her iPhone. Randall's words from the speaker were distant but clear: *"Off the books, it's your fee for keeping your mouth shut about the methanol deal."*

Randall shot up from his chair, his expression that of a vengeful god, and Sukiya stepped back, her phone held aloft like some strange device. "Not only does it record," she said, "it also e-mails."

Randall stood as though held by invisible chains, breathing heavily. Sukiya nodded, seeing he understood that his incriminating voice now occupied some unknown bit of cyberspace.

"My pen," she said. Randall picked up the Tibaldi

as though his hand had arthritis and passed it to her. "Don't worry, Randall. Don't worry. We'll face the coming storm together."

Still holding her phone up, she walked to the window and hoisted herself onto the inside ledge, wriggling back into the recess. The marble was cool under her thighs, the city was spread beneath her, and the green-grey sea rippled beyond. Sukiya felt the warmth of the tropical sun through the thick plate-glass as she leaned back. She opened her legs. "Come, Randall," she said. "Come kneel before your mistress."

IVORY KELLY

This Thing We Call Love
Belize

E ven though I was only ten years old, I could see why women loved Raymond so much. Raymond was tall and muscular with smooth black skin, and he had neatly kept dreadlocks that reached down to his waist. Once, when my Aunt Debbie was at our house, I heard her say that Raymond was a handsome Mandingo. Later that evening, Raymond was walking past our house as my mother was plaiting my hair on the verandah, and, talking partly to myself and partly to my mother, I said, "Hmm, that Raymond is *one* handsome Mandingo." I heard the sound even before I felt it—a dull *klop* as my mother cuffed me in the head with the back of the comb. The thing I couldn't figure out, though, was why Raymond's wife loved him so much. Miss Pauline was my mother's best friend, and she came to visit my mother almost every day. Each time she came she lamented how badly Raymond treated her, and about the many sweethearts he had. I suppose it was because of Miss Pauline and Raymond that I became curious about man-and-woman business.

One Friday evening, I was studying my spelling words on the verandah when Miss Pauline came bustling toward our house. Her eyes looked wild, and her bushy, half-Spanish hair swung violently from side to side. Her fleshy hips, miraculously squeezed into a pair of yellow polyester shorts, also rocked and bounced in a feisty, belligerent manner. Looking up the street past her, in the direction of Cinderella Plaza, I could see that the hatch window of her panades shop was propped open halfway—a signal to her customers that the place would be opening soon.

"Vangie, which part Florence deh?" she asked me as she approached our yard. I could tell there was trouble between her and Raymond again.

"Ma, Miss Pauline come look fu you!" I yelled over my shoulder.

Many times I had heard my mother say, "Why don't you leave that no-good man and go bout your business? All your children done big and gone on their own. You don't have to put up with Raymond and his schupidness." But Miss Pauline never listened. My mother was the kind of person who didn't tolerate foolishness, but somehow she never seemed tired of listening to Miss Pauline's troubles.

My mother came out onto the verandah, and I moved halfway down the steps with my spelling book, even though I knew I wasn't going to get much studying done until Miss Pauline left. "What happen, gyal?" my mother asked as the two of them settled onto the wooden bench on our verandah.

"That Raymond gone too far this time!" Miss Pauline declared.

"So what happen now?" my mother asked, half bored, half interested.

"I hear him talking to the uhman on the phone."

"Which one?"

"One from States. Yes! The man have American uhman now."

"You mean a white uhman?"

"I don't know, Florence. White, black, or blue, weh difference ih make? Uhman is uhman, and that no-good one got *my* husband. Ah hear Raymond with mi own two ears yesterday evening, talking to the uhman on the phone."

"Was she calling from States, or is she here in Belize?"

"States. And from the way Raymond was talking on the phone ih sound like ih met her while tour-guiding at Altun Ha."

"Yap; that sound like Raymond, all right."

"But that's not half of it, Florence. Ah hear dem making plans."

"What kine a plans?"

"Raymond planning to go to States with this uhman."

"But how man so facey, eh!"

"Ah hear the uhman telling Raymond that she will

send money to pay for his passport and plane ticket and everything."

"But *how* man so facey," my mother repeated. Even though my back was turned to her, I knew she had put her hands on her hips. "And how come you hear all this, Pauline? You mean to say Raymond was talking to the uhman on *your* house phone?"

"Yes; that's how facey Raymond facey. He was acting suspicious, so ah went downstairs into the shop and hollered to him upstairs: *Raymond! Ah gwine lock up shop early this evening fi go see Mama.* Mama wasn't feeling too good, you see. And ah mek plenty recket in the shop, slamming the windows and doors shut so Raymond would think ah was locking up. Then ah hollered to him again: *Raymond, ah gone!* And ah slam the gate hard and walk up the street. But then ah swing right back and sneak into the shop quiet quiet. Then when ah hear him talking upstairs, ah pick up the phone line in the shop. And that's when ah hear his whole conversation with the uhman. You know, it just goes to show, you can't trust dem tourist uhman these days. Plenty a dem come to Belize fu more than just the Maya temples and the Caribbean Sea."

"But what you mean bout tourist uhman, Pauline? You know that when it comes to your husband no uhman safe, tourist or no tourist."

"That's the God's truth," Miss Pauline conceded, "but you just wait and see. Ah will fix he business good one of these days."

"Cho, Pauline. I hear you say that a thousand times. I don't know how you love suffering so. You know, you remind me of my mother."

"How comes?"

"Gyal, you well know how much outside pickney my father had, God rest the dead. That man had pickney with a uhman in every district, plus he had one in Panama while he was working down there on the canal years ago. Even after he get old my father still had sweetheart; but my mother never left him. Of course, in those days most uhman does have to just grin and bear, as they say. But nowadays uhman have more choices. Take you, for instance, Pauline; you making your own money, all your children grown and gone, plus you still look good and could find another man easy easy. But still you putting up with Raymond all these years."

Eventually my mother and Miss Pauline went on to talk about other things such as politics and the price of goods going up again at the shops—my mother, being a loyal PUP, putting the blame squarely on Prime Minister Esquivel. But every now and then Miss Pauline would steer the conversation back to Raymond, or to men in general, and my mother would say, "Uhm-huhm; that's how man stay." My mother and her friends' conversations were like boil-up, with plantains and cassava and other kinds of ground food and salted meat thrown into a pot of water, in no particular order, and boiled until the pot is a steaming, bubbling, savoury cuisine.

Two weeks later, on a Saturday evening, my mother

sent me to buy panades at Miss Pauline's shop. About two dozen customers were gathered in the small yard space in front, some of them reaching all the way onto the street side. I jostled my way through the noisy crowd and headed toward the counter, the smell of fresh coconut oil and fried corn making me hungry. Someone was shouting, "Hurry up with my panades, man, Pauline, I hungry bad!" David Ramsey, who was in my standard four class but was small for his age, was yelling at the top of his high-pitched voice: "Miss Pauline, mi ma say please send two dollars salbutes and a dollar garnaches! She will pay you later!" Having almost reached the counter, I wedged my way in front of Mr. Lalman who was shouting, "Three dollars panades, Pauline, and I want plenty peppa!" I noticed the flask of white rum jammed into his back pocket, and I wondered how strong rum mixed with hot pepper tasted.

I ignored the noise and tried to make eye contact with Miss Pauline. It was a trick I had taught myself at the fish stall on Barrack Road. The stall was always crowded and noisy, especially on Friday evenings, and I used to notice that the people who made the most noise were usually ignored. Now, when I finally got Miss Pauline's attention, I said, "Mi ma want three dollars panades, Miss Pauline."

"Right now, Vangie girl. I will get to you in a minute." She said this in an extra-sweet voice as she wrapped a pile of panades in a piece of shop paper. The paper quickly became soaked with hot oil as Miss Pauline pushed the greasy package across the linoleum-covered countertop toward Mr. Lalman and collected the three dollar bills from him. Then Miss Pauline paused and cocked her head a little to the side. That was when I noticed the noise coming from upstairs. Something fell heavily on the wooden floor above the shop. Then came the sound of furniture being dragged across the floor. Then there was another loud thud, and the sound of angry footsteps walking briskly up and down. Miss Pauline had a triumphant look on her face.

When I got back home, I handed my mother the panades and said, "Ma, I hear big ruction upstairs at Miss Pauline house, like somebody turning the place upside down." My mother threw her head back and let out a loud, girlish laugh—the way she used to laugh before my father went away the previous year and got locked up in a Texas prison for entering the States through the back. Now, I was curious to know why my mother was laughing like that, like she knew what the ruction at Miss Pauline's house was about. But I had to pretend that I wasn't interested in big people's business, otherwise my mother would stop letting me hang around when she had company.

My curiosity was satisfied when Miss Pauline came to our house the following evening and described to my mother how Raymond nearly went crazy when he couldn't find his passport and wallet. "You should-a see how the man had the house looking like hurricane just pass through," Miss Pauline said as she sat across from my mother on our worn living-room sofa. "Remember how ah tell you that the uhman from States was sending money for Raymond to buy his plane ticket and things? Well, on top of that Raymond gone and withdraw all the money outta his credit union account; every single copper! But yesterday morning ah find his passport and wallet hiding underneath the chest of drawers in the bedroom. Ah tell you, Florence, the wallet thick-thick so with money." She indicated the girth of the wallet with her thumb and index finger. "So ah tek the passport and wallet and hide them somewhere else. And that's how come all day yesterday Raymond was turning the house upside down trying to find them."

"And did Raymond ask you anything?" my mother replied.

"Ask what? And admit that ah ketch him fair and square? Not him! Raymond would-a rather eat sand than admit that ih get ketch. Raymond would-a look mi straight in mi eye, and he would-a act so poor-thing-fied and innocent, swearing to God that no, he and the uhman is just friends, that ah would start to wonder if maybe he is telling the truth and it's me and my jealous ways that's causing all the problems."

My mother said, "That's the worst thing about it, though, Pauline—when you start doubting and blaming yourself like that."

It wasn't long before Miss Pauline tried another scheme. It was one of those things that big people do in secret. But on Murray Street, where the houses were so close you could borrow an onion from your neighbour by merely reaching over your verandah railing to receive it, there was no such thing as a secret. David Ramsey told me about it on our way home from school one evening. He said that Miss Pauline had been going up north to see an obeah woman. "The obeah uhman fix it so that Raymond is of no use to any uhman," David Ramsey said. I found this puzzling because Raymond passed by our house almost every day, and he looked no different to me. When I pointed this out to David Ramsey he burst out laughing and said, "Hie-ya-yie, gyal. You better ask your ma that one."

Miss Pauline went to stay with her mother for a couple weeks. When she came back, she said to my mother: "I don't know why I can't leave Raymond; I try, but ih hard. To tell the truth, ah wish *he* would leave me. The other day ah even begged him to. *Begged* him. But ih wouldn't budge. I know that sound strange, me begging mi husband to leave me."

"No," my mother said. "Ih no sound all that strange at all. This thing we call love is a very tricky thing."

"I never tell you this before," Miss Pauline continued, "but sometimes when ah going through all this sweetheart business with Raymond, ah start thinking all kine-a things. Bad things. Like how ah could-a throw a big pot of boiling water over Raymond while ih sleeping. Mek ih pay for all of the hurt and shame ih put me through. Lately ah find miself playing out the whole thing in mi head when ah lie down in bed at night. Ah think bout how easy it would be to just get up, walk into the kitchen, and put on the pot of water to boil. More and more ah find miself planning out things like that and feeling crazy-like in my head."

"That's why, Pauline, you have to leave that man," my mother said. "You doing all these things to try to get revenge on Raymond; but what you doing to yuself is far worse."

I stayed on the verandah for a long time after Miss Pauline left that evening, thinking about things— about Raymond and his many sweethearts, and about my grandfather who had a woman in every district, plus one in Panama. I wished I could ask my mother about such things, but my mother didn't tolerate children getting into big people's business. She thought I wasn't paying much attention to the things she and Miss Pauline talked about, but I was. I wondered what kind of husband *I* was going to have when I grew up. Would he be like my father who made my mother laugh like a girl, and who the Americans put into their prison for trying to make a good life for his family? Or was I going to marry a man like Raymond who had many sweethearts and caused a lot of misery and pain for Miss Pauline? But mostly I thought about Miss Pauline, about how she was beginning to feel crazy-like in her head. And it frightened me.

PART II

Gods, Guns & Ghosts

BARBARA JENKINS

A Good Friday
Trinidad & Tobago

n later years, when he lying in bed all by himself, Y'boy KarlLee lose plenty sleep wondering whether he should've put a raw egg white in a glass out in the sun that midday. Then he does catch himself and think, well, maybe knowing beforehand wouldn't a been much help to him that Friday when he first set eyes on Sunity.

When Sunity walk in the bar that first time, the whole room stop, just so. People didn't turn they head. They didn't stare at she. They simply freeze what they was doing and saying, and slope a low-down eye over, tracking she where she passing. Y'boy KarlLee thinking that if she did think she could slide in here and blend in easy-easy, without anybody paying her any mind, well, it only go to show she either too green for words or not quite right in the head. But look she there, right in the middle of the barroom, causing this sudden hush, everybody antenna up, and she? She cool-cool, too far inside to turn away and walk back out, even if she did notice the effect she having.

And if she wondering if she make a mistake to come inside, who could've blame her for choosing this place as a refuge? From the outside the little bar look so cute and inviting, just the kind a place someone in her position would choose to escape to. Look, the name *De Rightest Place* alone announcing that you reach where you should be. Them words sprawling above the outside doorway in a wild double cursive like if a fanciful child write it, twice—first in red paint, then alongside each stroke, like a sunshine shadow, in yellow paint. Each letter of every word, from the *D* in *De* to the *e* in *Place*, sprouting flowers and leaves from they tips and making curlicue vines with hybrid combination of flowers—hibiscus, allamanda, bougainvillaea, passion flower, ixora, heliconia—plus animals: giant black bachac, blue-and-yellow macaw, green iguana, brown cricket, yellow crapaud, stripy snake, tessellated morrocoy, translucent gecko—all kind a thing scrambling, hiding, preening, perching, all down the side of the sky-blue street wall as if some crazy flora-fauna mutation had scramble up from the flower bed below with its sole intention to reach all the way to the top, the better to hug up and love up the words.

Hanging just to the side of the door is a board, where you could read in stark black on white, the who and what and when and why of De Rightest Place. The sign saying in bold capitals taking up a whole three lines: *INDIRA GABRIEL LICENSED TO SELL SPIRITUOUS LIQUORS ANY DAY, ANYTIME.*

It wasn't any day—it was Good Friday—and it wasn't anytime—it was four-oh-five in the afternoon—and Sunity, in her Good Friday church clothes—black sheath dress with a wide, white satin, pleated cummerbund, black fishnet stockings, black-and-white patent leather high-heeled shoes, black pillbox hat with white grosgrain ribbon and black spiderweb fascinator—would've stop traffic anywhere, even in St. Michael's and All the Archangels at the Stations of the Cross vigil where she just come from, on any day, especially on a Good Friday.

Them stiletto heels beating a plink-plink-per-clink on the terrazzo floor ringing through the room, like Rudolph Charles in the panyard signalling Desperadoes Steel Orchestra with his iron to come to attention to start the tune, the plink-plink-per-clink marking time to her rhythmic advance to the bar, where customers angling aside, guard-of-honour styling, to allow her space; Indira looking up, controlling amazement, while pouring out into a tall glass with the gold harp logo a steady, rising, creamy, foaming, black Guinness; Herman, releasing a shower of small change on the counter near a waiting customer and glancing down at Apocalypse at his feet; the rottweiler herself staying quiet-quiet, nobody know she right there, waiting for hint of provocation to unleash, she staying there, lying on her side, but tense black eyelids now flip wide open and blacker ears twitch sideways; Herman on autopilot, slipping off a left sandal and rubbing a calming bare foot along the bitch belly as he jerk his chin in Sunity direction and Sunity place some folded notes on the bar in front of her, saying, "A tall merlot on crushed ice, with a slice of lime, please."

He, Y'boy KarlLee, hear the voice. Afterward, when we heckling him, we say he "heed the call." Its authoritative diction, precise enunciation, and modulated pitch register in every listening ear, is true, but according to Y'boy KarlLee, it pick him out special, tunnelling into his own ear canal and startling his brain in a frisson of . . . he can't tell—all his years and years of experience can't tell him what. And then, as suddenly as her presence had conjure it up, the spell of silence break in an embarrassed outburst of excessive volume. KarlLee, jerking out of his stupor, slam down with undue force the domino he poised to play, Anil slug the last of his Stag and bang the empty beer bottle on the mosaic scarlet ibis adorning the tabletop; Amber and Fritzie take up, more loudly than they would've like, the thread of the whispered conversation they having bout Precious, Fritzie's contentious teenage daughter—yes, she of the powdered neck—and the room return to something like its earlier, indifferently welcoming state.

She step across with her drink to the nearest empty table and perch at the edge of a spindly wrought-iron chair as if she fraid to sit too far back. Under his eyebrows, KarlLee watching her crisp profile as she flip up the fascinator onto the crown of her hat. She bend over, looking into her glass, and, as her hair swing forward, a thick black curtain hiding her face, he turn his attention back to Anil's play. Y'boy trying to convince himself she not his kind a woman. Too cool. Too sharp. Too sure. But is he, only he, continuing to steal glances her way, who is the one to notice when her elbow jolt against the table edge, the red drink in her hand spilling over the rim of her glass and onto the immaculate white cummerbund.

See how fast Y'boy KarlLee bolt up from the dominoes game, sprint to the bar, grab a club soda, and in two-twos reach her side! He pull up a chair, drag out a handkerchief, pour club soda over it, and raise a quizzical eyebrow in her direction. All that action, and she not looking at him yet. Her gaze fix on the handkerchief he holding toward her. He, taking her slight shrug of the shoulder as assent, begin to dab, to pat, to stroke, to rub at the stain on the white satin, and under his hand it fade from red to pink to blush. Under his hand, too, he feeling the rise and fall of her diaphragm. He thinking her breathing coming faster and faster as he work at the stain. He feeling the warmth of her breath flowing through his hair, tingling his scalp, as he bend over her lap. She not so cool, after all. She not so cool. He could smell the fragrances of her, her skin, her breath, her hair—cinnamon, coconut, peppermint, vetiver, and oh, Y'boy KarlLee can't tell which is which, only it warm and nice and sweet—and he there, wrapped in the cocoon of that air, drinking it in, swallowing it, in and out, in and out. He rub and stroke and wipe at that cummerbund as long as he could and when the stain not fading further, he stop and look up at her face. He see her eyes red, like if she was crying.

"He died for us. He died for all of us." Her voice coming out as a whisper he have to stretch his ears to pick up.

He say, "Who?" But immediately he catch himself, and he suddenly feeling stupid, thinking, but not saying, *What the fuck. Damnit. Fool me.*

"Jesus," she say, in that soft voice again. "Jesus. He died for all of us."

"And that's why you crying?"

"He died." She say it like if the shock and horror of it only now hit her.

KarlLee get throw a little off balance, but he not a long-time smooth operator for nothing.

"You know, he died a long time ago. Years and years ago. Thousands of years ago." Y'boy surprise himself at how gentle he sounding—patient, slow, repeating, as if he talking to a lil child.

"In church today, I felt as if it was happening right at that time."

Y'boy stare at her face good. It looking real, real sad, the tears now flowing in two smooth lines down her cheeks. He thinking it remind him of raindrops as they slide off a banana leaf and he glance down, feeling a lil bit embarrass at that sentimental picture coming into his own cut-and-dry head. She still not looking at him as she carry on talking, soft-soft, as if to herself.

"I was there with Him, suffering with Him, at each station of the cross."

Jeezanages, KarlLee thinking, *what have we got here?* But discretion overtake the thought and he say instead, "You're feeling better now?"

"I prayed to Him to allow me to share His suffering. And He did."

For one tortured moment, KarlLee feeling she going to open her palms and show him a pair of bleeding stigmata and then what he could do? Club soda can't fix that. But the moment pass. Her hands stay fold up in her lap. He look at the delicate brown hands, smooth, catching the light like a fresh nutmeg shell. None of that false plastic nail and scandalous multicolour pattern paint on, like Amber and Fritzie own. These little nails only have a slight gloss, nothing else. He well distracted but she not noticing that. She keeping on with her story.

"Collection time was coming up. I was kneeling. I reached for my handbag on the bench behind me. I took some notes from the wallet, put the wallet in the handbag, rested the handbag back on the pew bench, and continued my meditation with my eyes closed, praying for oneness with His pain. I was so deep in meditation, I didn't notice the collection basket pass by, and the notes, my offering, stayed in my hand."

She open her palm. KarlLee look at it. KarlLee want to read her fortune there. He want to read if his fortune tie up with hers in the faint delicate tracery there. He want that little hand to hold his, tight, like she did hold onto the collection money. But, in that situation, what else Y'boy KarlLee could do but nod? Bout the going-to-church thing, bout the meditation-and-praying thing, he well understand. He use to go to church regular when he was a college boy. He reflect that he had to go to church then, no argument, dress up in white long-sleeve shirt with blue school monogram embroider on the pocket, white long pants, black leather shoes polish so bright you could stand up next to a girl and place your foot just below her skirt, look down at the shoe-mirror, and see . . .

"I placed my hand on the bench behind me to reach for my handbag to put back the money until the end of the vigil when I could hand it directly to Father, but when I patted and patted the bench behind me, I felt nothing there."

Shit, think KarlLee. "Oh no!" he say, but he looking at the way her round bosom rise when she stretch out her arm demonstrating the patting action on the invisible bench. And her arm, smooth and firm and gleaming and . . .

"I turned round and my handbag was gone."

Bugger, come in his mind. "Gracious heavens!" come from his lips.

"It had vanished." She raise her head. Is first time

they two head level and Y'boy KarlLee see her face, properly. She pucker her red lips something like a kiss, something like a Marilyn Monroe kiss to be exact, and then the lips blow out, *phew*, a puff of air. "It had vanished, just so," she say. So maybe it wasn't no kiss for him, but when KarlLee see the face, the eyes, the lips, well, he smile, because she nice. She nice, too bad. All he want to do is stroke that cheek, kiss those lips, feel those eyelashes tickle his body . . . but he catch himself quick. He have to show interest in the conversation.

"You saw who was sitting behind you? Someone who could have taken your handbag?"

"There was a couple I had noticed earlier. A man and a woman. In the first hour of the vigil, they were there, but at the start of the second hour, when I realised the handbag had gone, I looked for them and they were gone too."

"So they must've taken it?"

"I thought Our Saviour was testing me. Sending me a taste of His passion, which He would stop when He saw I had suffered enough."

She living in the real world, or not? What kind a person go looking for suffering when it have plenty round to partake of without conducting a search, eh? He himself have more than his share of suffering these past dry years—all a them people who does make foolish joke bout male prowess and say, *Red man always in season*, never include him in any survey, nobody never asking him how he making out lately. But she, she like a angel, maybe she is one of them angel come down from heaven to help mankind. KarlLee want to be the mankind this angel come to take in hand, take in that cute little hand. *Oh God*, he close his eyes, *that would be so, so sweet*. She talking bout passion—but he know bout passion, he is the passion expert, he didn't forget passion, even if is a long time since he taste any. And boy, oh boy, he could give this angel a taste of his passion anytime, any day. KarlLee can't open his eyes, he fraid she could read his mind with those impious thoughts next to her innocent words. He nod to let her know he still listening.

"I prayed for the second hour, thanking Him for my anguish. In the third hour I heard a rustling in the pew behind me and when I shifted my position to investigate, I saw the man and the woman, the couple who was there in the first hour, kneeling once again in the pew behind me."

"So, did the handbag come back too?"

"There was still no handbag. The test hadn't come to an end."

"Did you get it back later?"

"After the third hour, the vigil ended and I went out to my car. It wasn't where I had parked it. I wasn't sure if that was another test, so I looked for it in case I had mistaken my parking spot. Most of the cars drove off and mine wasn't among the few left."

"The car keys were in the handbag?"

"Yes. And my house keys too."

"Your driver's permit was in your wallet?"

"Yes."

"The insurance certificate in the glove compartment?"
She nod.

"And, of course, your home address is on both."

"Yes, plus my cell phone with all my contact numbers is also in the handbag."

"You went to the police station to make a report?"

"No. I was walking round in a daze, but when I saw the sign I came in here, De Rightest Place, to settle my mind. To help me figure out if this is my test, to give up everything I have and follow Him as He bid us do. I even gave up the collection money, in exchange for the wine."

"Look, Miss . . ."

"Sunity, call me Sunity."

"Look, Sunity, first things first. By all means, give away all you own, but don't encourage people in stealing it."

"So, what you suggest I should do?"

"Let me take you to the police station to make a report. Afterward, we can figure out what to do next."

She look at him a long-long while. KarlLee say later he feel he was going through a exam he hadn't prepare for and, while he willing to take a guess in a multiple choice, he didn't know what subject he was being examined in. She look at his hand, fumbling on the tabletop, it still holding the handkerchief, stain pink like the cummerbund stain, she look at his face, now flushing even redder through the red Chinese-Payol-African mix-up creole skin, she look at the eyes, into them greeny-amber up-tilt eyes that earn him the school-yard nickname *Cat Eye*, and she must see something there that she like, because she stand up and touch her hand to his own.

They leave the bar together and all the hush and the sly glances that greet her when she walk in come back again. On the pavement outside, KarlLee hearing the excited buzz rise up in the bar and he know they talking bout him and her and he wishing it could have something for them to wag they tongue bout and who knows, maybe, if he could play his cards right in this next stage, who knows what it might lead to. They gone to the police station in his car, the little red Mini Moke bachelor convertible KarlLee assemble his own self from a kit he send to England for. Every nut and bolt he put in, and anybody who ask him, *Where you buy that car?* he say, *I make this car myself. I didn't buy it.* So, they gone to the police station and afterward he offer to drop her home to make sure everything all right there.

The little red Mini Moke turn in her street and she say, "Look. That's my car there. In front my house." KarlLee see a black Sunny park up in front a white house and when he reach it, he park up too. She open the gate, it not lock, they go up the path to the porch and he see that the front door wide open too. She go first and walk in and when he reach the porch and make to follow, she hold up her hand and stop him from coming in. Standing in the porch, he could still see what going on inside the living room. She squat down and she say, "It's all right, Lucifer. I'm home. What you've been up to, eh?" He see her patting and rubbing a big-big white pit bull who only smiling-smiling, jaws wide-wide, showing more rows of teeth than one a them great white shark. She concentrating on the beast, but Y'boy KarlLee scoping out the room over her head and he spot a nashy little feller crouch down on the floor, next to a mahogany glass cabinet, covering his head with his two long skinny arm. She stand up and the dog stand up too. If you see how that beast big, it wide like a young bullcow. She and the dog walk toward the feller by the cabinet and she say, "Stand up. You're a man, so stand up like a man."

The feller stand up, but his head hang down. He looking at the dog, who not doing nothing threatening, he only standing next to the woman. "So, where're my handbag and keys?" The feller try to talk, he try to point, he try to look in a direction, but is like he hypnotize by the beast. He can't do nothing. She put her hand on the beast head and the dog sit down next to her. She say, "Where's my things?"

The feller say, "K-k-k-kitchen."

She leave the beast and slip past a counter and she come back with a handbag, the exact match to the black-and-white-stripe patent leather shoe she have on. She open the handbag and look inside. "Keys?" she say, and he reach in his pocket and pull out two big bunch.

They jangle-jangle in his hand, like the Angelus bells, he shaking for so. She say, "Rest them on the cabinet." She say, "What's your name?"

He say, "P-P-Prakash."

She say, "Prakash, I want you to deliver a message to those people in the church, the ones who sent you here in my car, with my handbag, to rob me. Tell them: Lucifer leads you into temptation, but when you sin, he doesn't let you out." She looking straight at the feller, but he not looking at her at all, he only looking at the dog. She put her hand on the beast head and she say to the feller, "And you remember that too. It's not too late to change your ways. Go. Now!" The feller move slow-slow, scrabbling sideways, eyes bulging out he head like a mangrove blue crab, out the front door, down the path, out the gate, and then pelt speed down the road.

Y'boy KarlLee mesmerise too, by the scene, by the events, by the dog, by the woman. She stare at him. She say, "Come inside. It's over now. Let's relax." She sit down on the sofa, she lean back on some cushions, and she pat a space next to her, "Come on." He go inside, moving toward the sofa, but he too looking at the beast. She see that and she say, "Lucifer, here." The dog come and she bend down, hold his ears, and tell him something quiet-quiet, and the beast walk out the room and flop down on the floor in the front porch, right in the doorway. Lucifer put his head between his front paws and watching them like they is just a movie.

Y'boy KarlLee kind a relax now too and he go and

sit down on the sofa next to her. She say, "How bout some red wine?" and he see that she smiling right up, right direct into his face.

He smile back, broad. He say, "That sounding just right." He pause and carry on in that offhand way he have, "But you don't think you should take off that nice dress first?"

She look at him in a sort a way like, *Where you coming from?*

He say, in his flip, kind a cool way, "Well, we wouldn't want another accident to happen to it, would we?"

She laugh. "Accident? What accident?"

Y'boy KarlLee point at the faint stain on the cummerbund.

She say, "Oh, that? Yes! Oh, yes. Ha ha ha." She laugh, he laugh, they laugh.

She kick off them spike-heel shoes and send them flying across the floor. She lie back on the cushions, close her eyes, and let a long sigh escape, "Aaaah." Then she snuggle deep into the sofa, moving her whole self into a kind a slow unwinding dance. She raise her arms above her head, she point her toes, stretching the arch of her foot, KarlLee watching the calf muscles swell and tighten; she push down her heels and the top of her thighs rise, pulsing rounded mounds straining against the black sheath dress. Point-push, point-push, point-push. But Y'boy KarlLee don't unwind. He can't unwind. He get wind-up instead. He completely transfixate on the action, he two eye trap in the fishnet stockings, in the diamond mesh self, as it stretch open and close, open and close, like the mouths of fish beached in a seine, his brain lull into a trance under the sighing susurrus of his hot red blood, surging from one chamber of his heart to another, forcing open the valves, closing them, in syncopated rhythm with the point-push, point-push, point-push. She pause in mid-point, she turn her head slow in his direction, she half-open her eyes, and she say in a kind a dreamy murmur, "Ummmm, I could do with that glass of wine. Stay here, I'll be back in a minute."

And Y'boy, Y'boy KarlLee, he stay there, stranded at the edge of the sofa, gasping like he just get tumble by a Maracas wave, waiting, waiting under Lucifer impassive gaze.

SHARON LEACH

All the Secret Things No One Ever Knows
Jamaica

I

Ten years ago, I found out that I wasn't my father's only girlfriend. For years I'd been hearing my mother accuse him of screwing around on her. I'd always believed she was talking about me. After all, he'd told me I was the only woman he ever needed. What did I know? I was fifteen; I believed him.

What happened was this: There had been an uprising downtown, that day in September 1998. A popular area leader and enforcer was arrested and carted off to the Central Police Station on East Street, a few steps away. His loyal supporters hurriedly organised an angry protest by mounting roadblocks, looting offices, and harassing people doing legitimate business downtown before converging in front of the station demanding his release.

My father's girlfriend operated a beauty salon on East Street, smack-dab in the middle of this craziness. The shop came under attack by a group of rowdy area toughs who held up the staff and customers at knifepoint and robbed them. Thank God, nobody was hurt and the boys fled after they'd gotten the loot. Later, when things quieted, my father was able to rush to the salon. Marshall, his driver, who had taken me to a dentist's appointment in Half Way Tree, instead of taking me home as he was supposed to do, had chased in the opposite direction, back downtown, to see if his help was required.

My father owned a top-rated construction company that had erected the complex that housed the salon. Now, in the underground garage of this building on East Street, I felt vulnerable and scared. Rather than staying in the car as I was instructed, I followed Marshall, hurrying, afraid I would lose him. And then, there it was. Marshall, my father, and a woman standing by a pedestal chair beneath colour posters of black women with elegant processed hairdos. My father still had his sunglasses on.

I was just in time to see the woman—well, girl, really; she couldn't have been very much older than me—slap him hard in the face, theatrically, comically almost, as though she were some movie actress. I froze where I stood. My father was a real Jamaican businessman, which meant that regardless of how refined he was on the outside, inside he was a street fighter.

I couldn't imagine anybody taking that kind of liberty with him—my mother knew better than that—let alone such a young woman. She was a tiny thing, good-looking in a cheap kind of way that kind. She had too much of everything: yards of too-black fake hair, too much makeup, too-big boobs, too-long acrylics. Too much.

I waited for the fireworks. None were forthcoming. My father just stood there watching her sadly, like a puppy whose chew toy had been taken away from him.

"You just coming now, Raymond?!" she screamed at him. "You just coming? *Now?* Dem hold us up and rob we! An' you jus coming now?"

Then she launched herself into his arms and suddenly they were kissing, deep and greedy, and he was rocking her back and forth. Neither of them noticed, until it was too late, that I was loitering by the door.

On the drive back home I caught Marshall watching me in the rearview mirror. How long had he known about this girl? What other dirt did he have on my father? Marshall was a former amateur boxer who'd fallen on hard times; my father had admired him and was giving him a break. I held his gaze. He wouldn't tell me anything, though, even if I begged him. I knew enough to know his lips were sealed—in the same way I knew he would never tell my father about us. That we'd gone to his flat on two occasions after he'd picked me up from school. That the only thing he'd allow me to do was give him a blowjob. That after both times he'd emptied himself into the palm of his hand and blubbered like a little bitch, "Jesus, you're just a child," before promising we'd never do it again.

He was watching me in the mirror now, waiting for me to tell him whether or not to detour. I imagined his erection straining against his pants. But I turned away without a word. My stomach felt queasy. I kept picturing my father kissing that woman. That kiss wasn't just a kiss. That was the kiss I wanted him to reserve for me.

II

I hated eating dinner with my parents. Back then, my mother still insisted that the three of us dress and eat dinner together, carrying on the charade of being a regular family. This was non-negotiable, the one area where my father insisted we give in to my mother. He told me this one night as we snuggled in bed, his arm around my middle, his mouth latched onto my breast like a greedy baby. "I'm the only man who will ever satisfy you," he'd just whispered to me. "We're cut from the same cloth." Then he told me about my mother's dinner request.

Who were we trying to impress? Who were we fooling? Dressing for dinner made even less sense now that my two older brothers were no longer at home. I missed my brother James especially. He was the one closer to me in age, the one I'd grown up playing with when we were children, then followed around when he'd become a moody teenager. Then I'd become a teenager too, and we'd again grown close. He'd always made dinner bearable by making faces across the table, or joining in, as if it were a game, when I rolled my eyes.

That evening, when my father sat down to dinner he refused to meet my eyes. It was the same way he'd ignored me earlier that afternoon after realising I'd found out his secret, before bluntly telling Marshall to take me home. I would have preferred carrying up a tray to my room and chatting on my private phone line to my friend Sigrid about the guy I'd met earlier that day until we had to hang up and start our home-work. Some kids would be sitting at the table nervous from the strain of trying to act normal, from trying to decide how their loyalties should be split. But, no, my loyalty was always with my father, to him alone. I was used to keeping his secrets. And I wasn't twitchy or anything from what I'd found out about him earlier that day.

"I'm starving. Something smells good," he said to no one in particular.

My mother beamed as though she'd cooked the meal herself. She had never cooked a meal in her life. She was a former Miss Jamaica contestant who'd gone straight from her mother's house to my father's. "Doesn't it smell good? Adele made her world-famous rum and black pepper–glazed filet mignon."

She nodded at Adele, the squat weekday maid, who hovered worriedly in the doorway.

"Mm," my father grunted, digging into the tenderloin. "Excellent, Adele," he said, glancing up after a moment. "As usual." My mother looked rebuffed for a moment, disappointed at not receiving more of an acknowledgment for at least coordinating the dinner.

"Well, don't fill up too much," my mother soldiered bravely on. At forty-two, her looks were nowhere near beginning to fade. She was still slender beneath the long dress she wore, and her long black hair, which she tied in a low ponytail, had only a few barely noticeable strands of grey at the front. Turning her green-eyed gaze toward me, she said, "There's chocolate ice cream for dessert. But if your mouth feels sensitive, sweetheart, you can have cheesecake. You can have cheesecake, can't you, baby?"

"My mouth is fine," I replied, rolling my eyes. The eye-rolling was now almost involuntary. "It was just a filling; not an extraction. And I hate cheesecake."

"Well, I can ask Adele to—"

"It's fine. I'm not even hungry. I don't want dessert."

My father cleared his throat and aimed the remote control, which was resting on the table beside his wine glass, toward the family room. On the TV, the newscaster, who wasn't very au fait with her use of the English language, was reporting on the disturbance downtown earlier that day.

My chair scraped against the brick floor and I found myself on my feet. I stood there for a while glaring at my mother. I wanted to tell her that I thought she was stupid. I knew things she didn't. She didn't know these things because she was too busy being pretty, just some rich man's concubine, a man who was screwing another woman. What kind of wife didn't know these things? I would have made a better wife for my father.

Throwing my napkin down on my plate, I stormed off. "Leave her alone, Camille," I heard my father say, sighing wearily before turning back to finish his dinner. "Just leave her the fuck alone."

III

Upstairs in my room, I fell onto my bed, staring at the head of the lizard that was peeking out from behind the painting on the wall above the bookshelf. My father standing up for me at the table was nice, though I craved so much more. I'd always understood that our relationship had to be a secret. But everything was fucked up now I knew there was someone else. People would never understand our relationship, that it transcended the laws of society. It wasn't as if he was some creepy pervert who fooled around with his daughter. He'd been coming to my room since I was twelve but he'd waited until I was ready, when I got my period, before taking our relationship to the ultimate level. Which other man would have shown me that consideration?

I flipped on the TV. The eight o'clock news on the other station was about to start. They were leading with the downtown story too. I pointed the remote at the screen. I didn't need something else to remind me about my father kissing that girl.

I reached for the phone and pulled it onto the bed beside me. I started to dial Sigrid's number, and then hung up. My mouth felt weird from the filling and I was suddenly very tired, not in the mood to talk. Sigrid was the daughter of Spanish expats who went to the international school I attended. She was the only person I knew who was as smart as me and who possessed a similar sense of humour. She was my only friend, the only person I trusted with private, intimate details of my life. The private, intimate details of my life I wanted her to know, the ones that weren't off-limits, that is.

After a while I got up and sat at my desk. As the computer booted up, I scanned my notebook and realised there was still a pile of homework. I didn't mind. Actually, it was weird, I loved homework. But tonight it wasn't homework that interested me. I dug into a pocket of my book bag and found the business card I'd put there earlier that day. It was cream-coloured with embossed gilt letters that read simply: *Ronrico "Rick" Anderson. For Private Security.*

In the bottom corner was a phone number. Earlier that day at his girlfriend's salon, my father had called the police station and, because of his influence, a detective was dispatched there, almost immediately. After the detective had taken a statement about the robbery and passed out business cards, my father looked him straight in the eye and said, "From now on, I expect you to check in here as often as possible." Then he handed him a thick brown envelope.

I knew, of course, it was a bribe.

When the policeman, a youngish muscular guy dressed in jeans and a Michael Jordan jersey, brushed past me as he was leaving, I put a detaining hand on his. "I'd like one of your cards too, officer." I said it in a flirty way, tipping my head to one side and raising an eyebrow. I don't know, I felt bold, as if seeing my father with his girlfriend had changed something. I pictured myself in bed with him.

I sat at my desk now, trying to conjure up the policeman's face. He was cute. Sexy in a working-class kind of way. I wasn't one of those girls who had a particular type: if the package came with a fairly nice-looking face and a working penis, I was good. Thinking about being with him, I knew, was wrong. And not because he was a grown man—it wasn't as if it would be my first time with an older man. It was wrong because Ronrico "Rick" Anderson was a cop, and a girl like me simply wasn't supposed to shit outside my social circle. But I figured if my father could do it, then so could I.

I slid down in the chair and pulled my panties down around my ankles before making my fingers blades and sticking them between my legs. Ronrico "Rick" Anderson had looked speculatively at me, standing there in my school uniform. I was tall, with a curvy body that men, if they didn't bother to look at my face, tended to mistake for a grown woman's. I closed my eyes and

remembered Ronrico "Rick" Anderson furtively glancing over his shoulder to make sure my father wasn't
watching before he stuck his business card in my hand.
My fingers moved urgently as I tried to block out the
sounds of my parents arguing, focusing instead on the
feeling of pleasure that was shimmering on the horizon. I imagined Ronrico "Rick" Anderson's big hand
squeezing my neck as he pushed inside me, his breath
warm against my ear as he whispered dirty things.
I wasn't the kind of girl who read Danielle Steel
romances; I wanted a man who would violate me, do
to me what I imagined my father did to Mignonette in
bed. I smiled, excited by the smutty look I'd seen in his
eyes, and his willingness to betray the man who'd just
put him on the payroll.

IV

Sigrid and I spent most of our senior year obsessing
about colleges. I stayed over at her house on week-
ends and we would lie in her bed, smoking cigarettes we stole from her parents' bedroom, with Fifi,
her Jack Russell, panting excitedly between us as we
went through brochure upon brochure trying to decide which schools could best accommodate us both.
When we'd started thinking about advanced studies,
we hadn't been 100 percent sure what we wanted to
do with our lives or what we would study, but we had
a general idea. Now we knew what we wanted. "Defi-
nitely not Ivy League, the pressure is way too much,"

Sigrid would say absently by the window, blowing stealthy smoke rings outside, steering them away from where her mother's yoga circle downward-dogged in the garden below. I wanted to go to a school with a good English department, one that also offered a diverse set of extracurricular possibilities. Sigrid was more of a Renaissance type of girl, who was contemplating some kind of combination of her two loves: science and music. Her parents were returning to Spain at the end of the year and although they wanted Sigrid to attend school there, they'd agreed to let her choose the place she wanted to be, which was wherever I was going.

My parents, meanwhile, didn't care where I went, just so long as I was going somewhere. To say they were overjoyed that I was going to college was an understatement. My brothers, who were both just as smart as me, maybe even smarter, had squandered everything. Stephen, the eldest, had dropped out of school, even before he turned eighteen, and shacked up with his form teacher. We'd heard Casey had kicked him out after a few years and that he was smoking crack on the streets downtown. What my father had never talked about was that Stephen spent most of his day on a cardboard bed along with other dropouts in a burnt-out building across the street from his girlfriend's salon.

Then there was my brother James. Jimmy, whose elevator didn't go all the way up to the top floor, had been expelled from more local schools than my parents cared to remember. Finally, they'd sent him away to Florida to a school for children with behavioural problems. He had been there only one semester when a junior at the school reported that Jimmy had sodomised him. Of course, there was a lawsuit and everything, an out-of-court settlement, and Jimmy had returned home in disgrace.

And then, just when things couldn't get any worse, Stephen had come home one day and killed himself in my father's study.

A normal family might have used these kinds of crises to band together. But my family and normal didn't share the same PO box. We drifted even further apart, our secrets stretching tightly between us.

Meanwhile, nights, I waited for my father in my room. After he ate dinner he'd disappear again for hours, returning in the wee morning, long after my mother had succumbed to her wine-soaked dreams, dead to the world. My room felt cavernous, filled with the scent of an occasional early-morning breeze perfumed by jasmine, and my longing. I was alone, limp with fatigue, staying up long after I'd finish my homework or studies, fighting sleep while listening for his footfalls on the staircase just outside my room, which he had to pass before reaching his, which was at the end of the hall. I tensed, waiting for him to pause at my door before softly turning the knob. But he would increasingly pass by without stopping, leaving me exhausted and with dark circles under my eyes the following morning, and causing my mother to cup my face in both her hands and remark, more than once, "You're studying too hard, sweetheart."

The more he pulled away from me, the more I reached for Rick. I pretended he was my father and allowed him to do to me in bed all the things it would take to keep him with me forever.

But what did I know about forever? I was, by this time, almost eighteen; still a child, although I didn't believe it then. I knew about forever in the same way I knew about love, which was not at all.

Sigrid and I had narrowed our applications down to a few schools in the States, with Cornell University my number one choice, although I didn't tell her. I was no longer sure I wanted to go to school for another four years with Sigrid. I was excited to be heading off on my own—I even began yearning to leave Rick— and I realised I wanted a clean break from everything that reminded me of Jamaica. Sometimes it didn't seem possible that I could be so unhappy, considering how much I had compared myself to other kids my age, and believe me, I understood how extremely lucky I was. But there it was. Sometimes things didn't add up.

V

I started college in 2001, thinking everything would be different. I was mistaken. I was homesick, sure, but the foreign students always are. To make matters worse, the pall of the terrorist attacks hung in the air like a shroud. After the initial rallying together in the face of a national trauma, things silently returned to the status quo, the mistrust of foreigners. It wasn't exactly the best time for foreigners to be in New York.

Incomprehensibly, one of the people I missed the most was one I'd been in a hurry to leave behind. When I told Rick I was going away to study, he'd been upset but there was nothing he could do. I was beginning to feel suffocated by him and couldn't pack my bags fast enough. It wasn't that I didn't like him. I did; our relationship was exciting. There's nothing better than secret sex; I'd never been able to have any other kind. But Rick kept acting as though we were a normal couple—he threatened me with violence when he knew I was with another guy—as though he couldn't have been brought up on charges as a sexual offender if my father found out what we were doing.

In those first weeks on the campus, however, I missed him, and I maxed out my credit cards on plane tickets for him to come up so we could be together almost every weekend.

When my father was finally confronted with the bill, he was furious. "Who the hell is this man you've been screwing?" he shouted at me over the phone. Across the ocean I could hear the single ice cube in his Glenlivet hit the side of his glass.

I was thrilled that he was jealous. "You don't know him," I taunted. I remembered Troy, the boy from my class I'd dated for a week in my senior year, just to see what his reaction would be. I'd invited Troy over to study with me in my room every evening. At the end of the week, my father had come into my room and told me that if he ever saw another boy there he would kill me.

"Sweetheart," he said now, his voice low and soft, the voice I hoped he used only with me, "you mean more to me than my own life. You know that. I know these past few years have been, well, I know you've felt abandoned—you know why—but I *love* you." He was flying to New York the following week.

I met him at his hotel in Manhattan one chilly October night while rain misted down in the streets. Beneath my trench I wore a black leather catsuit that had a zipper up the front. I'd packed an overnight bag that contained sexy new La Perla playthings that I didn't even wear for Rick.

When I called up to his room, a woman answered. I knew her voice instantly.

He was still Mr. Movie Star. He wore tan leather boots, a sports blazer, and his jeans tight, as though they were a second skin. As though he didn't know how sexy *effortless* looked on a man his age.

His eyes slid down my body when I took off my coat, and his hand rested on the small of my back as we followed the maître d' to our table. All through dinner I kept waiting for him to tell me that he'd taken his girlfriend along with him on the trip. He didn't.

Conversation was desultory. I was moody and I wanted him to know I was pissed off.

When our dessert appeared, I said, "Why are you even here?"

He looked at me and put down his fork, squared his shoulders. "Your mother and I are getting a divorce. I wanted to tell you in person."

I stared at him hard and long. "Is that why you brought that whore with you? Am I going to be introduced to my new mommy?" Then I said, "I thought you wanted me in your bed again."

My father did not break character. He cut off a piece of cheesecake. A tiny piece of crust had landed on his moustache. He brushed it off deliberately. When he spoke, his voice was cold. "What are you talking about?"

I stared at him, finally understanding. He wasn't here to tell me he was divorcing my mother. He was here to dump me. "All these years, I told myself that what we did was my choice," I said, and stood up. "I know what you did to Stephen and Jimmy. You did the same thing to me. I don't know why I convinced myself that you and I were something else. You're a sick piece of shit."

My father watched me pick up my leather Louis Vuitton weekend bag. A sly smile played around his lips as he looked pointedly at it. "Sweetheart," he said, taking another bite of his cake, "if I am, then what are you?"

VI

Every family has its secrets. Mine had more than seemed possible. On the day my brother Stephen killed himself he'd come upstairs and knocked on my door. His eyes were wild but he was lucid. "Hello, kiddo," he'd said, and smiled broadly. Of all of us, he was the one who most resembled my father. Even now I'm embarrassed when I think about how I'd recoiled when I smelt his body odour. He'd handed me a letter and asked me to give it to my father when he got home.

After he'd broken into my father's safe and shot himself with a gun he found in it, things happened fast. The letter had been stashed away in my desk and forgotten until I was packing to go to college. It was addressed to my father but I'd opened it and read how it had started with them, how my father had gone into Stephen's room and sat on his bed and spoken to him like an equal. When his body had cooperated—this is what haunted Stephen all his life—my father had made him feel complicit, made him feel as if he was the one who'd asked for it. And, worse, my father had done the same thing to Jimmy.

I'd ripped up the letter and flushed it down the toilet, refusing to believe what I'd read. But I knew the truth, even if I didn't want to acknowledge it: my father had seduced all his children in exactly the same way. I was not special to him at all.

VII

Rick and I were in bed at the motel where we'd met two or three days a week for the last few years since I came back to Jamaica. I'd just told him that my father was finally going to marry his girlfriend, and that he'd told me I had to move out of the house. "You understand, sweetheart," my father had said. "She wants to start married life without any baggage. Anyway, it might be a good time to get off the gravy train. You need to find a job. Getting out on your own will be good for you."

There's no such thing as water under the bridge. *Forgive and forget* is just something pipe-dream losers, helpless victims, hang onto because they're unable—or unwilling—to do anything else.

I told Rick this, and he agreed with me.

"You know what turning the other cheek gets you?" he said, smiling just a smidge so I'd know there was a punch line waiting in the oven.

I smiled back at him, waiting.

"Bitch-slapped on the other cheek."

He reached over and kissed me, pleased with himself. This was one of the reasons I liked him so much. He was the only person I'd ever told who my father really was, yet he didn't act as though I was some damaged little bird, which he knew I would hate. I wasn't some pathetic victim like my brothers. Like my mother. Rick hadn't even made me feel like a loser when I'd returned home after being expelled from Cornell in my sophomore year—a bit of foolishness, which I never spoke about—and was bumming around, doing nothing, depending on handouts from the man I hated more than anyone else in this world. Of course, I did not tell Rick how I yearned for him—my father, that is, even now—and was unable to imagine what my life would be without him when he was gone.

And he would be gone.

Ronrico "Rick" Anderson promised me he would.

Ten years ago, downtown Kingston hadn't quite yet become the complete social and political clusterfuck it is today, with its diminished-seeming offices, burnt-out buildings, dilapidated storefronts, sleazy wholesales, and zinc-fronted, graffiti-ridden holes-in-the-wall behind which people actually live.

The day before Rick shot my father to death when he made his customary early-morning visit to his girlfriend's beauty salon, traffic had streamed down East Street. Overhead, sullen clouds drifted by like bits of gauze.

I parked across the road from the salon and stared up at the window, trying to imagine what the day after tomorrow would be like. But I couldn't. All I could think about was tomorrow, and hope it would be a perfect day for a murder.

JOANNE C. HILLHOUSE

Amelia at Devil's Bridge
Antigua & Barbuda

*On an island nobody ever really, truly disappears
without a trace. No, what we have here are bodies:
a woman found in the bushes in All Saints, a tourist slain at Darkwood, a girl washed up at Devil's
Bridge . . .*

    *They're few and far between. That's why they
make the news, because it always kind of shakes us
up that there might be someone among us who could
do such a thing.*

    *But there are no places to hide bodies, nowhere
where they won't eventually reveal themselves.*

A thin girl crouches behind the flimsy cover of a cassi
tree when she hears cars, more than one, coming up
the path. She is naked and old enough now, at thirteen,
to be embarrassed by that. Her mind is a fog and she is
wet, as if she's been in the water.

Only that isn't possible, is it?

Somehow, she's at Devil's Bridge where the rocks are sharper than a coconut vendor's cutlass, and the waters lash with a vengeance. Nobody swims at Devil's Bridge.

None of that explains why she is wet and why, when she licks her lips, it tastes like salt, and why, when the water trickles down her back, it burns, as if there are cuts there she can't see. She'd done a little dance earlier, like a dog chasing its tail, trying to see, and aching for the burning to stop.

It was like the burn of a good beating, the kind she got the first time she'd run away. She thought Mammy was trying to strip her skin off her back that time; the way she sweated and screamed, her face ugly, arms flapping, as the belt wailed. Then Mammy had called out to everybody she knew: "You all talk to that gyal dey, you nuh, ca me'll kill she."

After the fourth or fifth time, the social worker told Mammy not to hit her anymore; that when she ran away again, Mammy was just to call them and let them handle it. Only they were short-staffed, and the police was "don' care ah damn"—Mammy's words—and with everybody looking the other way and her mother's hands tied, the girl knew she could stay gone for weeks if she set her mind to it.

But she didn't plan on ending up here at Devil's Bridge, which she only recognized because of a long-ago school field trip. How could she have remembered the route or hitched a ride, and why? She can't cut through the fog in her mind to get to the answers, and the cars are closer now, causing her to draw in even tighter behind the spindly cover of the acacia, thankful for the grey of foreday morning.

They pass. Bringing up the rear is a Nissan pickup loaded with things, manned by three boys, boys maybe a little older than she is, sitting on the very edge of the vehicle as it bounces up the path.

She tracks them all the way up to where the path ends and the land flattens out into giant slabs of bleached and jagged rock, and patches of thin grass. She watches as they unpack kites, of all things, and a cooler from the pickup, and turn up the stereo. Reggae blasts to wake up the morning. *"Sun is shining,"* sings Bob as the sun begins its lazy stretch into daybreak.

She stands near the back of the truck, so close she can see where it's starting to rust, her nakedness forgotten as she eyes the drinks in the open cooler. She's suddenly so thirsty. She thinks about asking for a drink, or maybe stealing one; it's not like they're paying attention. Thirteen or so of them, men and boys, all ages, and they're busy getting the kites in the air. No one will notice if she slips a Coke into her pocket.

That's when she remembers she doesn't have a pocket, that she's naked. And shouldn't the water on her skin have dried by now? She's shivering against the wind as it hits the droplets still running down her body as though she's only just stepped from the water.

And that's the other thing: she can't swim. Few can from her landlocked, dirt-poor part of the island. So it doesn't make sense that she would be all the way out at Devil's Bridge by herself to steal a swim. How did she get here? How is she going to get home? Maybe she could ask one of the men for a ride or, if they refuse, hitch a ride on the back of the pickup when they aren't looking.

Sure, Mammy'll be angry, probably beating-angry in spite of what the social worker said, but she'll be happy to see her too. She's always happy to see her.

"Why? Why you do these things?" Mammy always asks, and her silence makes her mother angrier. She doesn't know why she runs away; she doesn't have it any worse or better than anyone she knows. Life is rough but it's rough for everyone. She has food, clean clothes, a mother who worries when she doesn't come home; once she'd even had a father.

Warm feelings flood her as she thinks of that time, when Daddy would let her help as he fiddled around under the hood of his thirdhand Ford every Sunday, before taking her to Thwaites parlour for strawberry ice cream. Folks called her a daddy's girl, something that would make her smile so wide her cheeks would dimple. But then Daddy left, and Mammy got misera-ble, and now strawberry ice cream makes her stomach hurt.

When Daddy left she wanted to go with him, but he walked away and didn't look back. As much as it is possible for a person to disappear on an island as small as Antigua, he disappeared.

When she runs away, she doesn't go looking for him though; she isn't a stupid little girl anymore, and if he wants to be gone he can stay gone.

She doesn't want him.

She wants to go home.

She watches one of the men grab a length of string and run toward her, his eyes shining like stars, his grin splitting his face; it's the kind of joy she's only ever seen on the faces of kids too little to know any better.

She is crying outright now but the man doesn't seem to notice, he keeps coming straight at her. She dodges at the last minute.

"Hey!" she yells.

But he keeps running, and he is laughing now as he finally turns and looks up, slowing, stopping.

She yells again. But he just keeps right on, laughing and glancing up, and one of the other men walks over to him, pats him on the back. Together, like little boys instead of grown men, they look up at the kite. She looks up too. There are several kites in the air now. Some aren't even kites at all, not the newspaper, coconut bough, turkleberry kind. More like big-big balloons; and they are all kinds of colours and shapes, fish and squids and things. She stands, just staring for a while. It makes for a pretty picture, the too-bright colours against the spreading yellow of sunrise. For a minute it's weird; she's up there with them, straddling the big blue fish and riding the wind, and feeling like a cowgirl riding a steed like in those old John Wayne Westerns her dad used to watch late at night on Turner Classic Movies, back when she was a little girl, and he'd defy her mother and let her stay up late, and she'd fall asleep to the sound of hooves pounding, keeping time with her daddy's heartbeat against her ears.

She finds herself down in the dirt, and wonders if the man had run into her after all. She yells again to get his attention. Then, when he continues to ignore her, she starts jumping up and down, arms flailing like she is playing mas in carnival or something. But none of them look at her. They are flying their kites, drinking their drinks, none noticing the girl whose breasts are only just starting to come in, the girl only now getting hair under her arms and between her legs, the girl with tears running down her face, the girl whose throat hurts from screaming, the girl wet and naked right in front of them.

She screams then sits in the dirt like a two-year-old. But they never look in her direction. As they start to pack up, she grows desperate, doesn't want to be left alone up here at the eastern edge of the island, alone, not knowing how she is going to get home. So she runs ahead of them and squats down near the cassi tree until she hears the tyres crunching on the loose soil and rocks. At the very last minute she steps out in front of the lead car, a restored red Lada, and is relieved when the driver breaks so abruptly that the truck tailgating it bumps it lightly.

"Wha de hell, man, ah so you jus mash breaks?" the driver of the truck demands, stepping out.

"Me see subben," whispers the driver of the car, sounding spooked.

"Subben laka wha?" demands the one driving the truck.

"Me na know, like one naked gyal pickney."

The others step out of their vehicles to witness and weigh in on the melee and laugh. Still none of them are looking at her.

"You ah see t'ings, man," one scoffs.

"No, me t'ink me see um too," says the passenger from the first car.

"What would a naked girl be doing up here?" one asks sensibly.

"Well . . ." another begins, but is cut off with, "Man, get you min' out de gutter, ah wan likkle gyal pickney, not one big woman, and she look scared."

"You see she now?" one teases in a salesman's voice.

"Ha ha," the second driver snaps back sarcastically.

"Let's jus look roun likkle bit to make sure."

"Man . . ." more than one of them whines, but they spread out anyway.

Caribbean folk know that if the dead want to be found, they'll let you know where they are, and if they could talk they'd probably tell you who did it too. The dead are purposeful like that. By Devil's Bridge there's a hidden spot known as Lovers'

Beach, a shallow cove carved out by the force of the water. It's the kind of place a girl of thirteen has no business being at any time of the day. Much less with fractured ribs, which investigators say might have been caused by her body banging against the rocks before coming ashore.

But who can tell.

The dead don't speak.

EZEKEL ALAN

Waywardness
Jamaica

It Doesn't Get Much Better Than Gay

Brian had always been wayward; even as a child he seemed to be drunkenly tottering far from the straight-and-narrow and lunging recklessly toward the deviant and murky. He was gay—not in the love-having-fun-only-with-men sort of way, but the straighter gay. For him, it really didn't get much better than being gay. Every day for him was a romp, a frolic, a dalliance with desires and, occasionally, whores.

His was a waywardness that not even the Nazis would have had the extermination capacity to get rid of. Gas it! Auschwitz it! Cremate it! That shit would still be there, Tutsi strong against their Hutu machetes and cockroach chants. There wasn't a damn thing Brian's waywardness couldn't withstand.

Some people have bad habits that are easily murdered in relative secrecy—not Brian. His waywardness survived assassination plots by his ma, his grandma, his pa, his grandpa, and every rassclaat uncle, aunt, and neighbour who made it their concern. Some of those killers tried to take it somewhere in isolation, get it to kneel, shoot it in the head, bury it in a mass grave with the millions of other childhood habits that have fallen victim to homicide. Here's some that have been laid to rest in peace: "Courtney liked to steal from shops," "Tony sucked his thumb," "Thirteen-year-old Sharon was caught with an older man," "Wayne would grin like a nigga when they caught him unmentionably verbing his own sister." Whipped to death! Aloe vera mixed with sulphur bitters poured down the throat to poison it at the root! Murders committed on a massive scale by adults who then drank rum together and listened to the BBC World News. All those "I don't need to listen to anyone" nascent, wayward habits left reeking and decomposing in obscure, unmarked graves.

What couldn't be killed was imprisoned in some godforsaken place worse than Siberia, like a nasty, stinking, dirty, shit-and-use-your-hand-to-wipe-it jail in Pol Pot's Cambodia. Then forgotten, like bloody Chad. Ever heard anyone ask, "What's happening in Chad these days?" Same as, "Miss Loretta, what was it your daughter Suzette used to do again?" For-fucking-gotten!

Some habits, in tribute to their honour, put up a fight, while others did the most unusual (but perhaps smartest) thing at the start of a war—surrendered.

But not Brian's waywardness. This was no featherweight Chinese resistance movement; this would not be killed by tanks and regulations. Patriot missile it and then watch it apply for a visa to come and visit you. Nuclear bomb it and watch it mutate. It wasn't rassclaat going nowhere.

The Things You Can Be in New York City

Now, you could, of course, be wayward and live peacefully and anonymously in New York and other big cities. But could you get away with that shit in a deep rural Jamaican community? In the 1970s and '80s? In a place where farmers and their mules shared the same beliefs, and darkness described both people's complexion and intellect? I think not. Liking a pinch of salt with your coffee or preferring vegetables to red meat was one thing; but liking a man's buttocks instead of a woman's clit, or your daughter's instead of your wife's tits, was an altogether different matter. You could not get away with it!

You see, when you lived in a rural community such as ours, everyone knew your business, and if they suspected that you were "wayward," they'd be up in your ass about it. You'd be walking down the street and suddenly you'd notice people crossing to the other side, giving you the bad eye, cursing beneath their breath, and hissing their teeth. Some would start calling you names, others would be calling your mama names; or worse, boys would start throwing stones at your ass, and others would be stoning your dog and the chickens in your yard. Then you'd have to switch to wooden windows.

Do you, Mr. Peeking Through Half-Drawn Curtains, like touching little children? Brother, you'd better move to a city. You contracted HIV? There's a growing suspicion that you're gay, so make haste and relocate immediately! You are, in fact, gay? Beg for police protection as you relocate. You feel a special fondness for four-legged creatures? Shit, dude, leave! You like sleeping with your own daughter? Not even God Almighty can come down and protect you. Leave! Find a city!

One thing was guaranteed: if you stayed, you'd be dead.

You had to move to a city.

But not to *any* city.

I ain't shitting you, it was important to not only know what "ailed" you but also where you could be anonymous with it. Advice: You are a thief? Go to Kingston; you'll be offered your own section of the city to prey on. You're gay? You'll be just fine in Ocho Rios or Montego Bay; you'll blend into the woodwork. You're a rapist? Negril is for you; say hello to Donovan if you run into him and let him know his ma's unwell, but it ain't critical. If you have that soft spot for four-legged animals, then go to Falmouth; just remember that cows and goats are fine to molest, but people's dogs are off-limits—you'd be surprised at the things of little apparent value that some folks will kill for. Got that nervous, incestuous twitch? May the Good Lord bless and keep you! Pick your spot in a public cemetery and gradually pay down on a nice casket.

On issues of morality my cousin Trevor, after a particularly rejuvenating Pentecostal service, was most ceremonious in declaring the village position: "Brother, know thyself and know thy shit!"

One also had to be careful not to use trite expressions like *I am what I eat*, which you sometimes see people on Facebook joking about as they post a picture of a baby holding a piece of bacon in her hands with her pudgy pink face making her look like a pig. In our community, if it got out that you were in the habit of eating a girl's crotch or a dick, well . . . what do you think? As for *I am what I am*, I wouldn't go there. Just trust me on this. Case in point: Delroy. Of course, you wouldn't know my erstwhile neighbour Delroy. So anxious to see the world that he came from between his mama's legs like a bomb, the force of the explosion ripping her vagina, leaving her unable to walk properly for months. He came out alert, looking ready to walk, trying to talk, reaching for red meat, wanting to touch, nothing but bright-eyed curiosity. His willpower fierce, his courage firmer than a Congolese erection, people said he was born a man. The sad thing is, he was born in our deep rural community. When he was caught one cosy night showing extraordinary affection to another man, he offered in his own defence, "This is who I am, why can't you let me be?" Well, what can I say? That. Was. The. Rassclaat. End. Of. That. The nigga never even got the luxury of spending the rest of his life in sordid alleyways. (You are correct in guessing that he wasn't chased out of town and didn't get to ride off into some brilliantly orange sunset. The body that was found was headless; the message: If you can't learn, you must feel.)

This was, simply, not the kind of place for you to be wayward. Which is where it all went wrong for Brian.

Touching and Feeling

Let me tell you a little more about Cousin Brian.

He was a strange one, as I mentioned before, right from the very beginning.

Folks say that Brian came out of the womb feet-first, as if to test the waters. His little toes twitched, felt the coolness of the air, and sent back reassuring messages to his brain—everything was safe. He came in his own time, ignoring the coaxing and urging of both midwife and aunts; the fact that he nearly killed his ma during childbirth was part of the price to be paid for being born with his own convictions. He would, likewise, spend all his life trusting only his own judgments.

In 1976, the year in which I issued seventeen farts in a game with some other boys, Brian was nine years old and seemed to have finished developing mentally. While the rest of his body doggishly fetched nature's sticks, the boy inside remained resolutely nine, and he spent all his time grinning.

On his ninth birthday based on the lunar calendar—
which is nine months and seven days before his first
major theft, one year and seven days after his first con-
sensual sexual encounter, and one year, four months,
and twelve days before the first nonconsensual but still
very much sexual encounter—he was fully formed and
had all his limbs, fingers, and toes intact.

There were, undeniably, debates of great impor-
tance on the subject of the education of the children
of the community taking place during the PTA ses-
sions at the May Pen Infant School, but Brian's ma, our
aunt Bev, did not participate in any—this wasn't because
she was not assessed to have the required level of intel-
lectual curiosity, but because the school was unaware
of the existence of her child. Brian, therefore, grew up
without a proper formal education.

So, when he was nine years old—when Jimmy Car-
ter was still in office; when Jamaica was still Social-
ist; when Kristine DeBell was on the cover of *Playboy*
magazine; when Fidel Castro was up to his old tricks;
when Sputnik was already in orbit; when Brian was
slightly cross-eyed with jet-black hair, lived inside a
blue-and-white wooden house, suffered from asthma,
held a lizard for two weeks as a prisoner of war, and
called his favourite and only toy "the yard"—there were
four things the out-of-school child liked to do. The four:

Brian was always putting on all kinds of clothes—
for girls, boys, men, women—whatever he could find.
It was as though his life and identity were not yet de-

fined and he was searching for a therapist. He particularly liked the elasticity of women's underwear; jeans, and how they morphed into alluring sexiness when a woman stepped inside them; high-heel shoes; the ripe fragrance of worn, unwashed bras.

He spent quite a lot of his time manufacturing hoaxes; e.g.: he'd often run and grab Georgie's arm, smell beneath it, faint to the ground, silently mouth *Poison*, gag, then laugh at his own wit. And there was the cool smoothness of a piece of stone in his hand, the acerbic "Me going kill you to rassclaat!" response the same stone could elicit when it struck the back of a cousin's head, and the way the same stone could crash through a window and shatter both the dry and wet dreams of the night. He'd always laugh.

He liked to suck on soft fruits and his ma's breast. From all accounts he was particular to fleshy, squishy fruits whose juices dripped—sweetsops, custard apples, melons, hog plums, star apples, mangoes, and so on. He liked the feel of juices dripping along his chin, running down his skin toward his elbow, the sticky stains quickly removed with a lick, a slurp of his tongue. He loved the squeezing, licking, slurping, sucking, dripping of all of it. He would often get a Julie mango, slowly roll it in his hands, gently squeezing and softening it, then bite the bottom—the nipple—and suck its juice. It had to be nicely ripened for this. As for breasts, though his ma's were dry, and his ma had stopped breast-feeding him when he was six, and his pa didn't approve of the practice, and his ma wasn't always awake when he tried it, he continued to seek ways to suck on his ma's breasts. Other women's breasts would do fine, if they were willing, but they weren't always.

He liked to touch things that held mystery, that shone, that opened, that were soft, fleshy, wet, and moist. The sensation of plucking his fingers into fruits made him giggle with happiness. He sometimes plucked his penis into the same openings, and saw that this too was good. He took whatever he felt he needed to look at, to touch, to spend time with. There were no grand thoughts of wealth or accumulation. In truth, it never started as theft.

Salvation Is an Obese Woman

Walk, walk, slow, slow, look, look, touch, touch, walk. Wait. Wait. Look. Look. Walk, slow, slow, look, touch, walk. Wait. Breathe. Now!

Run! Grab! Run!

Run, run, fast, fast, run, run. Breathe. Breathe. Run, run, fast, run. Turn. Stop. Breathe. Run, run. Breathe. Run! Open! Open!!

It lock!

Bomborassclaat! Me dead to rass! Me's the Queen of England, me's royally and unmentionably verbed!

'Twas open! Me did check!

Lord, 'twon't matter shit if me try to give it back! Them won't care! Even if me cry and kiss them feet. Even if me ask fi forgiveness. Them won't care!

Them reach.

Oh Simone, them gonna kill me today!

Jesus Christ, them gonna kill me!

Them reach! Me dead! Me bloodclaat dead!

We Will Get It Out of You!

Brian raped a lot and stole a lot. Sometimes he got caught. The adults tried to help Brian the best way they could:

We'll have an intifada against that waywardness in your character! We will slaughter that lil' nigga!

We know what we'll do! We'll build a torture chamber and appoint a torturer—a great Mandingo out of Africa. He'll be the blackest, thickest, bowlegged slave driver from a seventeenth-century slave plantation, who uses the whip the way it was intended to be used, before those bloody British missionaries started preaching against it. And it will be a bloodclaat whip—"See it? Fear it? Has your name on it!"

We are going to bend you! First, we'll bend your ass over, then your rigid wayward character. Ooh, we will get it out of you for sure!

This is war! It's a tragedy for everyone; everyone suffers. We hate what we have to do, perhaps as much as you hate having a steel-toe boot rammed up your ass.

We are the faithful; this is an edict from no one else but God: Spare the rod and spoil the child. *This endeavour is crucial to the preservation of the species, to the rule of reason and morality. The enlightenment calls for it. Bring the whip!*

We smile only because we cannot cry. We can show no weakness. This isn't personal. It must be done; this thing must be bent into submission.

We all must suffer a little bit. But all things must pass, and as soon as this wayward spirit submits we can forget all about this. Start afresh, with nothing but tender, juicy love.

The Boy that People Saw

I call him Brian, but you can call him anything you please: dog, vulture, thief, nigga, jackass, idiot, mother-fucker (in either the vulgar or literal sense), liar, rapist—you can choose, just don't think that by abandoning "Brian" and using one of these it will make you some-how unique.

He was about sixteen in 1983, though no birth re-cords are available to confirm.

His religion depended on the grade of weed he was smoking at the time.

Now, allow me to introduce Brian. First, meet his left hand. This one had three fingers as two were lost on a special occasion—but not lost as in went walking and couldn't find their way home; they were chopped off by a butcher trying out a Muslim tradition.

Brian never went to school, he couldn't read, pic-ture books were okay when they were self-explanatory, and comics could sometimes be funny.

Our little youngster never fired nor even held a gun. He loved watching karate, which he often tried while laughing at his own silliness—"You killed my teacher!" was just about the only part he perfected, while squinting his eyes tight and putting on his best Chinese accent.

A couple of times in someone else's conversation he had heard reference to *university*, but he himself, believe it or not, never once used the word.

At sixteen years old there were countless regular words he'd never heard, some of which he was also likely to mistake if he had—like *ghoul*, which, with blissful ignorance, he would have associated with a sport.

Five feet seven inches, one hundred and thirty pounds, and generally normal but for a legion of scars all over his body. He had a round face with small crossed eyes which, when combined with his pointy nose and eternal grin, created a peculiar impression of one who suffered from perpetual astonishment. The gash beneath his lower lip was the deepest scar on his face and perhaps the sloppiest, and came, ironically, at the hands of a butcher who prided himself on his cuts.

"You think me handsome?" Brian once joked with his cousin Simone.

"Maybe you was handsome before God born," was her reply, which wasn't meant to be hurtful.

His shoulders were narrow and his head small. Slender, athletic, lithe, and dark—these were his most prized, God-given *talents*.

He smelled different from everyone—to be precise, unpleasant—and people noticed it. The scent was due to all the garlic he ate, combined with his infrequent baths and the residue of the catnip and peppermint leaves he rubbed on his skin at nights to repel mosquitoes. The baths were infrequent and also Navy Seal–short—they were taken in an outside bathroom close to the house and he had to be quick and alert in case some enemy, such as his pa, tried to spring a surprise and catch him for a good whipping.

At seven years old he had been the only child who, instead of peeing his bed, pooed it as he slept. As a toddler he'd often poo and try to outrun his ma to prevent her from changing his diaper.

He had no brothers, but two younger sisters who received their fair share of love and affection from their parents and also his.

In 1983 Brian's pa was a surly, middle-aged man, most of whose life had been based on imitation.

His name was Thomas.

For a while Thomas attempted to act like a real man, though the discerning would have detected more than a little hint of Yul Brynner in his manly mannerism, and might have confirmed their suspicion if they had known he had watched *The Magnificent Seven* three times during the week it opened at the local cinema. He was also renowned for his booming belches and lethal farts—a reputation consolidated after a dead cockroach was spotted beside his ass on a day that he'd let rip one of his most prized gas balls. No autopsy was needed to confirm the roach's cause of death.

Brian's ma, Auntie Beverley, might have been a licence plate numbered AB2222, noticeable for her plainness and sameness. Like a city without a proper sewage system, all her waste backed up in her fatty, greasy skin, and overflowed in her warts and bumps. She slept like a starfish, and she slept sound.

But the most interesting question is . . . well, what made Brian so interesting? The short answer to that is the fact that his waywardness did not appear to have been due to any specific turning point in his life—no rancour at once or twice being struck too hard by his pa; no resentment for being left, for the most, to fend for himself. Nothing. At least nothing that he could put one of his eight fingers on. Nothing he did was on account of spite, maliciousness, bitterness, or some feeling of being treated unjustly.

He and his family were shit-in-plastic-bag-and-dump-it-in-canal poor, but he never took a moment to reflect on it or think of placards and slogans.

The first time he was slashed badly was long after he had started stealing, not before. And though this had been agonisingly painful, he didn't think of it as unjust or cause for reprisal.

Similarly, his first time in juvenile penitentiary was fairly deserved, and wasn't on account of what was commonly seen as "police fuckery"—like when the pigs locked up a youth for smoking a little bit of weed and ruined his rassclaat life. Brian went where he didn't belong, took what wasn't his, and the running he was doing when caught was, in truth, part of the admission of guilt.

The only person he disliked was the man who bought his stolen goods, who he always felt was cheating him. He'd bring a brand-new colour TV for sale and get only enough money to buy four dinners and two hours with a whore at the Versailles.

Brian never once felt something stir inside him, egging him to rebel. He could remember quite vividly that when he was six years old and at his uncle's wedding reception, he'd stretched his hand for a slice of cake and was told to "bloodclaat leave it alone!" He took it, not because of a desire to disobey, nor a feeling of intense need. He simply felt he wanted it, and his pa's caution that he'd murder him if he touched it didn't seem like anything more than part of a conversation. When he took it, it wasn't to show that he could and, in truth, his urge to eat was also not particularly strong. His urge for sex, yes, was later clearly a problem. That was different and he knew it; something inside him felt strange each time that urge arose. "It feel like fire unda me skin, Georgie." He told Georgie everything. The rest of that story left Georgie with a deep-seated suspicion that Brian was the only person who cried as he masturbated.

As far as anyone could tell, Brian was heterosexual. Notwithstanding this:

Once, late at night, he'd found a house with a window loose, and though he hadn't scouted the property, he removed a few windows and then entered, pushing aside dusty, sun-bleached curtains. While no glass had fallen and he had scarcely made a sound as he worked, when he got inside the house a voice from behind said, "If you move, you dead!" The man told him to kneel. While holding a gun to his head, the man stepped in front of him, dropped his boxers, and gave Brian a full view of an instrument that had never seeded any form of life.

Brian managed to get a good look at the man, who was short and broad, about medium build, and shuffled when he walked. He was wearing brown socks with matching brown slippers. Both his boxers and mariner were once white but stained cream by sweat. His hair was thinning, and combed across his head to give the appearance of fullness. The oily sweat on his face— caused by a hot house in which he was too cheap to run the air conditioner—was of little help in concealing patches of peeling-dry skin across his forehead. It looked like some form of decay.

The Chiney man used his right hand to lower his boxers and then lift up his mariner slightly. The left hand held the gun. Brian saw other patches of powdery dryness on his belly below the navel and farther down on both sides of his thighs close to his very Chinese penis.

The man eased himself back enough for his ass to lean against a dark synthetic-leather couch, which was likely bought for its ability to conceal dirt and hated for the way it steamed the back of his legs and buttocks on a regular, let alone hot, day. This is how Brian came to see most clearly his only option to live.

Brian had sucked the Chinese man's dick, but from what he later told Georgie while playing, he was thoroughly repulsed by it—especially the horribly gaunt face and the tight popping veins in the neck that he looked up to see in the moment of shuddering release. He'd never forget the sour, thick, and sickeningly creamy taste of what spewed onto his lips. One might not have known just how disgusted he was judging from how he told the story to Georgie. He always laughed hard at both his jokes and misfortunes, sometimes reaching a voiceless crescendo, at which point he'd clap his hands like a seal. Those were some of the times he was most animated and seemed giddy and light-headed.

But he was never gay.

For the most part he preferred screwing whores, the often willing cousins and neighbours, and, much farther from home, the odd old woman or young girl he found walking alone through the bushes or backstreets of some town. He sometimes cried while he raped them, though this was neither an act of empathy nor atonement. He also slept with his cousin Simone a few times a week, and kept doing so even though he thought she was out of control. She screwed him hard, always wanting to be on top, screaming and making sounds unbecoming of an eleven-year-old who still lived with her mother. She was "red," which is to say of a much paler complexion than almost everyone else in rural Clarendon, had pinkish lips (if a boy had the same, he'd be accused of eating crotch), freckled baby face, and beaming bright eyes. She was always excited to see him, quickly ramming her tongue down his throat and squeezing his balls playfully. "You carry something fi me?" she'd ask. She liked to dress up in the stolen jewelry and clothes he brought her. He tried on her clothes. He liked her a lot.

Brian's pa, Uncle Thomas, had built a little bench by the side of their one-room house. At the end of a long day, after attempting to sell snow cones—which he succeeded in doing mainly on holidays and after the local schools had exams and the students wanted to celebrate—Uncle Thomas would go to lie there. At nights, this is where Brian slept—not because he was no longer welcome inside, but because he simply preferred the freedom. Brian liked to lie on his back, peer at the stars, and feel the coolness of the night air. Unlike the rest of us, he had no fear of anything living or dead. He told Georgie that one night he woke up and saw a demon. "When me open me eyes, me see one duppy standing over me. The duppy say, *Me is you, and you is me*," Brian recounted, then cackled at his own wit and at Georgie's gullibility. It had been a dream, and those weren't the exact words the ghost had spoken, but Brian also couldn't quite find a way to tell his best friend that he knew, somehow, that he'd soon die.

Brian was already gone in the early hours of the

morning when the rest of us kids went to catch water—and the worst of the watchman's temper—at a standpipe by the local Water Commission Office. We would see the piece of cardboard he slept on neatly folded. Sometimes there were cigarette butts, sometimes a black plastic bag that once carried the bun and cheese he had for dinner and which was now waiting to take the digested remains to the canal. But Brian was gone. He was not only wayward, but transient. He also knew that a man had to wake up and move before his doubts.

The Long and Short of It

Well, here's the long and short of it all, of Brian's story:

He grinned, he laughed, he joked, he raped, he stole, they caught him, they beat the shit out of him, he raped, he stole, he grinned, he ran, he jumped, he pinched, he raped, he stole, they beat him.

Twice they beat him days-of-slavery bad. And twice he died.

The first time was in 1983. Only Georgie cried.

He had pulled off another fast one, the details of which can wait, and was caught in the May Pen Market. The mob that caught him really beat the shit out of him that time. He died.

But he came back a few minutes later!

It was a genuine miracle! The faithful shepherds among us thought that he must, surely, have brought back from the "other side" all the knowledge needed to live a better life. After all, it wasn't everyone that got a second chance.

His mother, rumour had it, expected him to fall in love—"Him can even marry a nasty Indian woman, him just need fi settle down," she's reputed to have said.

In a school story I wrote at the time, I had him adopting a dog, with the two cutting a fine picture of perfection—one dropping poo in the park, the other sitting on a bench reading the Holy Book.

His closest friend Georgie feared he'd stop catching lizards and peeling their skin, and perhaps start to find meaning in the existence of the smallest things.

His pa, who'd always thought that every weapon he ever needed to deal with his son was natural and given to him by God (but who had given in to using a 4x4 and was increasingly tempted to further sin), now had visions of his son working in a factory.

When they scraped Brian off the market floor and washed away the blood that customers knew shouldn't be in the nonmeat section of the market, and counted him for dead—well, he wasn't breathing, was he?—all hope was gone. But when he opened his bloodied, swollen eyes, and faintly smiled, and took time to recuperate, and drank his mother's soup, and stayed home for weeks, and lightly touched the hands of those who came to visit, there was genuine hope.

Little did the niggas know that when Brian died he went straight to hell and found out that it was nothing but a hoax! There wasn't any devil, or even an identifiable figure of authority. All he saw was a bunch of lost and lonely souls searching for something. They looked the same as they did on earth, just shades darker from the heat. "And the heat didn't even bother me," he joked to Georgie some weeks later.

That was the first time.

One year later, he died again. The kicks were harder, the punches fiercer, the slaps firmer, the stabs deeper, and the machete chops . . . well, more precise. I was there on that day, with the rest, watching them beating and slashing him against the wall. If you were a foolish child you could have played in his blood as it spurted like water from a sprinkler. But I merely watched while they released the body and it crumpled to the ground, and life eased out of it like bubbles of methane from month-old cow dung. He had remained wayward, and this time he also remained dead.

HEATHER BARKER

And the Virgin's Name Was Leah

Barbados

saw a young woman being stoned to death on the thinnest strip of Oistins Beach. As I was walking home from synagogue, three young men were crouching in the sand, digging a deep narrow hole with their bare hands. They looked like dogs scratching around for somewhere to shit. Other men dragged the woman to the hole. She was screaming and fighting them off but they dropped some blows about her head before forcing her in feet first. She was about the same age as my sister, Leah. One of the men pulled a dark brown crocus bag over her head. But her hair—black, long, and lovely locks—spilt out. Another man packed sand in the spaces around her body while the other fellas strained under the weight of the concrete blocks they held above their heads. A younger man kept wiping his forehead on his upper arm. I was close enough to smell his sweat mingled with the scent of offal; maybe he scaled and boned fish in the nearby market. The mob looked over to an elder in a long grey gown. When he gave a quick upward nod, they dropped the blocks, one by one, on the woman's head. Her cries became gargles as her blood, almost black against the fading light, slowly soaked the crocus bag. When her head was twisted off to one side, the young men dropped the rest of the blocks and ran quickly into the excited crowd. An older woman sank into the sand. "Hadassah!" she screamed. Over and over.

I'd watched stonings of women before on TV with a sad curiousity. They were mostly for women caught in adultery. This was the first one I'd seen up close.

The elder's gown grazed the pale sand as he moved past the sobbing older woman, leaning forward to pat her head like she was a pet. She flinched. He stopped next to two uniformed policemen, there to make sure the sentence was carried out. They were skinning their teeth, pleased at a job well done. After all, they were obeying the law. The spectators left soon after; some on foot headed back to the fish fry, while others drove off quickly in their cars. Hadassah's mashed-up body stayed behind. It could only be removed by the gravediggers.

What would Rabbi Elkanah have thought? He was the person who reminded me most of God—loving, patient, real smart without making you feel dumpsy; an old man with a laugh that rattled his chest. He was reluctantly teaching me about the Levitical priesthood, unknown to my parents who thought I'd spent the past three weeks studying the Book of Esther. Anyway, Rabbi was always reminding me that women cannot be priests. After I'd worn him out with my "whys," I'd tell him that I should have been a boy. He'd laugh and say I would think differently one day. I responded as any teen girl would, by sucking my teeth and cutting my eyes.

When I got home my parents and Leah were in the kitchen talking real slow and quiet. I hid by pressing myself against the partition that led from the kitchen to the front room. There was a funny feeling in my belly. At first I thought they'd found out about my lessons. But then I realised Leah was doing most of the talking, which was strange since she was the quiet one out of the two of us. Then Mummy started hollering and Leah hollered back even louder. Next thing I know, Leah was saying something about being pregnant with the Christ child. My head started to hurt. The scriptures had prophesied that Christ would come from the line of King David in Jerusalem, not Barbados. And though we weren't living hand-to-mouth, it would be a stretch to say we were royalty. Daddy was a carpenter/mason/jack-of-all-trades, Mummy was a seamstress, and Leah was a nineteen-year-old university student with a harelip. And that brought me to the real issue: if Leah was telling the truth, then why her and not me? Okay, I was only fifteen but I was better looking and would have been a good king mother. I was also popular, recently inspiring girls in my class to let their hair grow wild.

After reading the account of Samson, I'd stopped combing and cutting my hair. My afro was messy but I felt stronger every day, and girls needed to be as strong as they could around here. We had little say in our day-to-day lives and even less in our futures. Last week one of the brightest girls had gotten married during lunchtime. No warning, nothing so. She was fourteen and hadn't come back to school. Our hair, though, we could control, even if only for a short while. Teachers nicknamed us the Bird's Nest Girls.

Leah, well, she spent most of her time with books and a Walkman. I'd not seen her around many boys. Maybe being pregnant with God's Son would make her popular.

She pushed past me into our bedroom. I moved slowly into the kitchen and, meeting the miserable faces of my parents, said, "Grandparents to the Christ. Nice!"

"Not now, Candy," Daddy replied.

Mummy shoved the pea husks she was shelling into a pile on the table and left in tears.

Leah was lying on her bed reading a textbook when I came in. "You hear what I tell Mummy and Daddy?" she asked.

"I was wondering why you ain't married yet. Makes sense now!"

Leah didn't smile.

"Seriously, everybody's waiting for the Messiah to come so we can have another king, like David. Things getting worse with some of these priests in charge."

"You believe me then?"

"Why not? You wouldn't bring this kind of attention to yourself. Unless you've gone off." I crossed my eyes and twirled my index finger next to my head. Leah grabbed a pillow and hit me. "For truth, I'm more likely to do something like this, not you. I always wanted to be looked up to. How you feel bout it?"

"Excited and scared. You done know everybody will be staring at me, thinking, *Why she?* I've asked myself that too," Leah said, stroking the dark shiny line above her lip.

After a few moments, I blurted out the question I really wanted an answer to: "So who you do it with then?"

Leah looked down into her lap. "That's the thing. Nobody."

"I don't get it."

"Me neither. It happened; I don't know how, it just did."

"So you still haven't done it?"

"No, of course not."

I had nothing more to say so I got on my knees and asked if I could feel the baby. Leah took my hand and laid it against the cotton T-shirt over her stomach. A minute later I'd still felt nothing and was about to get up when there was a small movement. "I feel something," I said, nodding eagerly, wanting to believe but reasoning that the flutter could have been caused by gas—not an unusual thing with us since feasting was so common in our family. Goods from Jerusalem came readily to Barbados, so the food I'd read about in scripture was easy to get on the island—olives, grapes, figs, arriving by sea with traders from West Africa or Rome. My favourite eat-up was the Feast of Tabernacles, which had ended the night before. I'd gotten to sleep in a tent that Daddy set up in the backyard. We remembered our forefathers who'd lived in tents in the desert and how God had protected them. But we also ate nuff food because the feast came at the end of the harvest season. Mummy, Daddy, Leah, and me had squeezed into the tent and tantalised ourselves with grilled steak, fish, salt bread, golden apples, pawpaws, and vegetables, as we gave thanks to God for what He had done for us and what He was going to do through His Messenger. Daddy bought pudding and souse, though we're not supposed to eat it. But pickled pig trotters, ears, and tongue could hardly be considered pork. Besides, it tasted so sweet that the risk of getting in trouble was worth it.

I moved my hand from Leah's stomach. She said nothing but looked happy. I was always striving, ambitious for a future, friends, and more things to be ambitious about. For truth, I was glad for my sister, but a part of me wanted what she had inside her.

Still, I wanted to share Leah's news with my friends at school. At lunchtime I limed with the rest of the Bird's Nest Girls. Vashti said her hair had grown by an inch, stretching a black wiry strand into the air as proof. Tamar pulled a comb out of her pocket that was missing most of its teeth; her mother had tried to tame her braided knots. I couldn't contain myself about Leah's pregnancy any longer, and pushing my fingers into my expanding afro, I said that she was carrying the Christ child. Most of the girls burst out laughing; a couple stared at me with narrowed eyes.

"Leah *is* pregnant with the Messiah," I repeated slowly.

"How you know?" Tamar asked.

"She tell me."

"I tell you the other day I was moving to Jerusalem but you never believe me."

"Leah don't tell lies, not like you," I teased. "Besides, it was foretold. It doesn't say who but it doesn't say who isn't. So it could be any girl."

"She did the thing? With God?" Vashti's face was screwed up in disgust.

"God don't have sex; He isn't married," I replied firmly.

"So how it happen, then?" Vashti demanded.

Her questions were getting on my nerves. After a brief but deep thought I said, "He put her to sleep and then took one of His ribs and put it inside her, you know, like Adam and Eve but backward." I had no clue how it happened but this seemed as good a way as any. Some of the other girls nodded. I answered the rest of their questions as best I could, making up what I didn't know or understand. So the baby was due during the Feast of Unleavened Bread, which was about six months away; his name was to be King David II (*Davy* to family and close friends); and my parents were thrilled to be grandparents to the Messiah. When the questions finally stopped Tamar showed me a note in her diary: *Christ child to be born in Oistins, Barbados, next yr, baby mother best friend's sis.* She slung a reassuring arm over my shoulder and squeezed.

Before the end of lunch I slipped away from the girls in search of Rabbi Elkanah. He was inside his office, a pile of books at either end of his desk. His large body filled the space in between. "You have something on your mind, child."

"Good news. I think."

Rabbi Elkanah tilted his head down and peered at me over the top of his glasses. I trusted him, not like some of the other teachers and scribes. Take Rabbi Phineas, for example. When I told some of the girls that our writing teacher had suddenly died (they thought he was a spirit when he eventually arrived in the classroom), Rabbi Phineas had lashed me with the metal buckle-end of his belt. He also forced Mummy and Daddy to provide a black-belly sheep as a sin offering instead of the pigeon offered by ordinary people. I did everything I could to avoid him but couldn't avoid his rules. Rabbi Phineas's nickname was 1,001 Commandments; every day it was like there was a new regulation. They were hard to remember and impossible to obey. The last time he came into our class, his strict handwriting had announced on the blackboard: *Thou shalt not look into the face of the Gentile and thy hands shalt not touch his, for the hand of the Gentile is unclean.* I glanced back at Tamar, whose arms had linked through mine many times, and gave her a flimsy smile. Her father was from Lisbon. Most of the Gentiles in Barbados first came on vacation from Europe, and then some returned and made the island their home because of the warm weather and friendly people. Some of the elders were saying that there were now more Gentiles here than the rest of us. Rabbi Phineas was harsh and controlling, but Rabbi Elkanah I trusted.

"Leah, she says she's carrying the Christ child," I finally explained.

"Many girls have claimed this, wanting a part in their own salvation. Do you believe her?"

My eyes began to water and I nodded slowly.

"Why are you crying, child?"

"Everything will change. Won't Leah have to move to Jerusalem and be queen? I won't see her again. She might forget me."

"If she has been chosen by Jehovah for this honour, she will not forget. I have prayed that I would see this day—the rule of the Holy One of Israel."

I dragged the back of my hand under my slimy

nose and stopped sniffling. "How we will know for sure? What scripture says about the mother of the Christ child?"

"Very little. But it does say He will come out of Bethlehem."

My heart started to pound. "Leah's supposed to visit Israel with her class. Next spring."

"Who else knows about this?"

"Mummy, Daddy—"

"Who else?"

"Some of my friends."

Rabbi saw the worry creeping into my face. He said sternly, "Leah is not married. If the High Priests hear about this she may not be safe."

I asked him what he was going to do, but he just shook his head and sent me off home.

The next morning I watched my parents loading sacks of spinach, bananas, breadfruit, and green mangoes into the car for tithes and peace offerings at the synagogue. Mummy had banned Leah from leaving home, so she just lay on her bed like a floppy rag doll.

"I wish it did you instead of me," she said softly.

I did too but thought better of saying so. "There must be a reason why. And it's probably for the best."

"God's so grand and mighty, why me?"

"Maybe because you don't think you're worthy; something as big as this won't make your head swell." My parents beeped the car horn. "Later, sis," I said, and blew her a kiss.

* * *

When prayers were finished I got up to greet a girl behind me, but Mummy grabbed me by my shoulders and steered me to a wooden bench. A man and woman, like my parents but older and dressed in purple linen, and a young man with seeking eyes and a serious face, stood waiting. The young man, whose name was Joachim, said nothing and kept his head bowed, though I caught him staring at my hair a couple of times. His parents did all of the talking, mine just nodded quickly, even when they said my hair was to be trimmed and combed. When my parents agreed, they all exchanged kisses. As soon as they left I looked up at my parents.

"Why you doing this to me?"

"It's for your own good, and for your safety," Mummy said. "When your training with Elkanah finishes at sixteen you will marry Joachim."

"I'm not ready, not yet. I want to study more and travel, find out who I am before I marry. Please." I tugged Daddy's hand and shook his arm.

He wiped his eyes with his free hand. "We ain't got no choice. People asking why none of we girls marry yet. And with Leah believing she pregnant, no man will want her. If one of you don't marry and soon, we may lose the inheritance," he said.

I had to think fast. "Suppose the stress of Leah's exams has brought this all on. You thought about taking her to the doctor?"

My parents did not tell me what they would do,

but I could tell by how they looked at each other that they were chewing over what I'd said. I asked them if I could walk home; I wanted to escape the memory of the gawking boy-man. I race-walked into the afternoon air. By the time I got to Oistins, sweat had soaked my underarms and back. In the distance I could see fish vendors hosing the raw stench from their sinks and packing up. On the beach, young Gentiles were scampering around in the sand in colourful shorts and swimsuits. The sun dazzled on the water like sequins. I reached for a pebble only to realise it was a piece of concrete block. I threw it away remembering the young woman who'd been stoned days earlier. I retreated into the shade and sank into the sand, the heat and weight of my betrothal heavy on me.

A lean man is standing in front of me. His face is shining, like Daddy's black shoes before he goes to temple. He is wearing a long gown and though his face has no wrinkles his shoulders are hunched forward. He starts to crouch down so I spring up, ready to run, grabbing a handful of sand to pelt in his eyes. But then he says my name. I relax a bit but my fist is still balled up.

"Let me cut to the chase: Your sister will give birth to the Christ child. He will be called—" the man pauses, "Immanuel, yes, Immanuel."

I nod, though I prefer Davy. "Who you are?"

"Just a messenger sent to explain the truth."

"So how this all happen?"

The man shuts his eyes tight, saying quickly, "As the Holy Spirit hovered over the earth when it was formed, He hovered over Leah until the Son of Man was formed in her womb."

"What about me? Who's going to hover over me?"

"You are to follow God. Leave the details to Him; just follow Him." He turns to leave before spinning back. "And tell your parents Leah has not lost her mind. A mental hospital in Barbados is not where the Son of Man is to be born; it'll not be much better than that though." He presses his lips together as if he's revealed too much.

Someone was shaking me. Startled, I woke to a little girl saying the water was creeping close to me. I scrambled up, dropping a fistful of sand, and ran home. When I went into the kitchen to get some water, I found a piece of paper folded in half on the table with my name on it. *Have doctor's appointment with Leah. Back soon. Food in oven*, Mummy had written. But I was not hungry. I went into my bedroom, dropped to my knees, and started to pray.

PART III

Mind Games

JANICE LYNN MATHER

Mango Summer
Bahamas

I t was a fruitful summer. People tend to forget that. Everyone was giving dilly away. The boys sold guineps at all the big intersections, straight from their hands. Dollar for a big bunch, then fifty cents, then twenty-five. Too many guineps to waste money bagging them. The boys pocketed the quarters and spent them on candy. No one made a profit. Sugar apples melted off trees and lay open on the ground, splattered buffets left for the rats. People were stacking up mangoes on the grass at the edge of their property to be taken away, and leaving unmarked brown bags of sickly ripe fruit on other people's doorsteps.

The air was slick with August humidity from the first week in May, and so tight with the smell it hazed orange. It did something to people. Abe Pratt, who used to beg bareback all morning and drink all afternoon, was so changed that, by mid-July, he appeared (sober) at New Roots Baptist Church's revival week in reasonably clean pants, a crinkled blue shirt no one knew he owned, and his hair trimmed so low everyone was surprised that his actual head was so small.

I was ten that summer. Theresa was eight. Both the perfect errand-running age, small enough not to talk back too bad, big enough to carry boxes to and from Sweet Mouth, who we were supposed to call Miz Liza even though no one else did, not even Mummy, when she forgot to be respectful herself or thought we weren't listening. The boxes went as fruit and came back as jam, twice as heavy. Theresa told Mummy this was because Sweet Mouth put ground-up rocks inside everything she made, and we shouldn't carry any more fruit to her to cook. And plus, didn't we have enough mangoes around already? Couldn't we throw them away? Weren't there hungry children somewhere around who wanted them? We didn't need jam.

She had a point. The backyard's sweet reek leaked through into the bathroom, because its window faced that side of the yard, so that it no longer smelled like soap or bleach or pee, as a bathroom should, but like a large, rotting fruit salad. The freezer was crammed with purée. All forms of dessert were suspected carriers. It was mixed into the pound cake. There were orange streaks instead of black flecks in the banana bread. Dinner rolls took on an unwelcome, fruity taste.

We weren't the only people on earth, Mummy reminded us. We didn't know what she was going to do with the jam. And why were we here, talking? Too much talking, not enough work. Hurry up, take those boxes, so Sweet—so Miz Liza can get them made up. And we better stay behind long enough to find out if she needs help peeling and dicing.

Theresa and I knew better. The jam would be with us every day for the next six years. It would cover our bread. It would sneak into our cookies, it would appear swirled into muffins, glaze baked chicken, replace cheddar in the macaroni cheese. It would be an integral part of our diets until Theresa or I got married, when Mummy would send us away with so many cases of mango jam there'd be no space in the new house for the husband. Perhaps, we agreed, as we turned down Sweet Mouth's street, the filled jars would have an accident on the way back.

We got to Sweet Mouth's house just as Nay, the girl from nine houses down, was leaving. Her wide-set eyes slid toward us, suspicious.

"Hey, Nay, you got cookies?" Theresa could pick out a sugar-filled foil package anywhere, particularly if it didn't have mango chunks in it. The crumbs around Nay's mouth suggested the package she held was of that sort. Nay said something that was probably meant to be "No," tightened her grip around the precious bundle with the earnest greed of a girl with four brothers, slammed the gate shut, and ran off. I set down my box so we could open the gate again while Theresa stuck out her tongue at the girl's back.

At the door, Theresa dropped her burden. "Miz Sweet Mouth!" she hollered through the screen door, in a way that would have infuriated our mother. Nudging her with my elbow, I banged politely on the wooden frame. Through the grey mesh, we could see the tiny woman washing a huge mound of plums at her sink.

"Brenda, that's hog plum she washin?" Theresa asked. I was sceptical too. No one washed hog plums in a sink. They were eaten outside. The seeds were spat out in the grass. They weren't even in season yet. No decent person had hog plums until late summer. It was May.

"Come in," Sweet Mouth called over the running water. Theresa opened the door, skipping in empty-handed. I followed, placing my box down on the floor. The kitchen was stickily hot, and smelled of syrup.

"What you makin?" Theresa asked, as Sweet Mouth scraped the small green fruit into a large pot. I rammed my sister with my elbow again.

"Miz Liza, Mummy say bring these to you for jam," I announced.

"Hmph. How many that is? Two boxes?" She stirred at the improper plums. "Go look in the dining room and see if I have any empty jars for this jam y'all want me make."

"What you doin?" Theresa was on tiptoe, practically climbing into the pot. Standing like that, she came up almost to the woman's shoulder.

"Boiling them for punch. Missy, you ain gone yet for those jars? Look by the chairs, I have some clean ones in there somewhere."

Scowling, I retreated into the dingy inner sanctum. How come I had to do the scary stuff? Theresa was the one always sticking her nose into things when she shouldn't. I scolded myself. I was older, I should be responsible.

"An' your ma pregnant again?" Sweet Mouth was asking in the kitchen. I hoped Theresa wouldn't say anything dumb.

I looked over the things on the dining table: a dog-eared phone book, a dusty vase with four plastic flowers, their petals thick and waxy-red. My eyes darted around the dim room. Sweet Mouth's white brocade sofa was covered in thick plastic, even though she had no children. No one had sat on it for years; it still looked new. I wondered if she was saving the sofa for something. On the floor next to it, in paper bags, were four huge plastic jars.

". . . new baby in October," I heard Theresa saying. I grabbed up the jars and turned back to the kitchen before she blabbed out all our family business.

"These?" I held the containers toward Sweet Mouth.

"Glass, girl, glass. You know what happen if you put hot jam inside plastic? Go look again. I need to send your baby sister to help you look?"

In the dining room again, I peered under the table,

then started back. Not only brown paper bags full of packages of sugar, but a huge spiderweb was woven from the wall to the table's front right leg. The dusty owner of the web skittered away before I dropped the tablecloth. Finally, my eyes lit upon a closed box next to the plain chair that stood awkwardly beside the table, its back pressed against the wall. I gingerly opened the box, and the rims of twelve jars winked out at me. I lifted it carefully.

". . . like little girls," Sweet Mouth was saying into the pot as I came back in. "Took you long enough," she said, her back to me. "Put them on the counter." Theresa was draining the last of something from a little pink cup. "Y'all go, leave me, let me do my work."

I dragged Theresa out. When we were a few houses away, I cuffed her in the back of her head. "You stupid, eh? What you was drinkin?"

"Coconut water." Theresa rubbed her head, glaring at me. "You just jealous you ain get none."

"You too greedy. Anyway, when you get poison, that's your business." We walked on another few minutes before I asked, "What she said about girls?"

"I ain tellin you."

I knew I'd get it out of her. She wouldn't stay mad long. She'd tell me that night, I knew, when we stretched out in bed, hoisting the sheet above us then letting it float down, falling light and cool over our arms and legs and heads, giggling over Mummy's half-hearted calls for us to shut up and go sleep. But I fell asleep first that night. And long before dawn, someone was banging on our window, yelling for Mummy to come, because Nay was missing.

We went to see Nay's mother, a lumpy woman who smelled of sweat and usually shouted a lot. The two mothers were great friends. "That girl was such a help to me. What you think this country comin to?" The mother's voice was strangely quiet. "House full a boys. What I go do? My one girl child missing."

Theresa and I exchanged a look. Nay was known for never missing anything. She didn't miss it if anyone opened a bag of chips. She didn't miss it if anyone had a new pack of Now and Later. Hand always out, always whining, "Oooh, gimmie piece?" And she had certainly not missed those cookies. Missing? We knew better.

We talked it over in bed, and decided she had gone off somewhere to a big party on the beach that we had not been invited to, with red and purple balloons and chocolate cake and sandcastles and plates and plates of Sweet Mouth's cookies. We fell asleep with the taste of envy sugary in our mouths.

I was sent to help Nay's mother hang out laundry first thing in the morning.

"Why her own children can't help her?" I muttered, shoving my feet into my slippers.

"You don't see the woman daughter gone?" Mummy glared at me, and it seemed like not such a good idea to tell her that Nay was really on her way back home, salty and sandy and full of dessert which we hadn't had. Nay's mother still had four boys who always had plenty of energy to throw pebbles at me when I went past their house. Mummy didn't look like she was in the mood to explain why they couldn't help, so I didn't ask. When I was done, I came back and lingered by the front door, waiting for Theresa, who was going back to Sweet Mouth's to collect the first batch of finished jam. She didn't look at me as Mummy raked the brush over her head. I pushed the door open and stood outside, where the air was moving at least.

"You wanna go down to the playground?" I asked as she came out.

Theresa plopped the empty box she was carrying over her head, shading herself from the sun. "Yeah."

"I'll go with you if you tell me what Sweet Mouth said."

"She ain say nothin." She grabbed up her box again and ran down the street, skinny legs flying. Nay's brothers celebrated her passing with a cloud of tiny stones.

Before anyone could spit up in the air and run, another two girls left. One I didn't know. Theresa was the other. They both went that same night.

They say three is the number of completion, so I'm glad she was the third to go. She knew it would happen, I think. But she didn't tell me that afternoon, just like she didn't ever tell me what it was Sweet Mouth said. In the nights after, when there was so much extra room in the bed and no one to talk to after I was sent there anyway, I went through seven or eight mundane possibilities before settling on, *Something coming what like little girls.* I could hear Sweet Mouth saying that. *Better sleep with one eye open. Better sleep in your ma bed. Something coming, something what like little girls.*

I like to think Theresa would have told me if she'd known she was going away for such a long time, though. Would have told me at least that night. Held my hand as we dozed off. But she didn't. Her last night at home was uninspiring. She lay on her belly, one arm thrown over into my side of the bed. I had been asking her, "So you ain go tell me what she tell you?" steadily, every three minutes for about fifteen minutes before I realized how regular and quiet her breath had become. When I sat up and looked at her face in the light coming through the half-open bedroom door, I saw she was half-smiling, her head turned away from me and toward the window. She was dreaming.

And then there was sleep, and then screaming, except now close, and what was far away was the fist banging on someone else's window yelling, "Come quick!" and it was Theresa who was gone.

I like to think her dream was a sweet one. She, being gathered up in soft arms, an even softer breeze kissing, kissing, kissing her forehead, kissing, kissing her nose. She must have known that Sweet Mouth was right, that there was something what loved little girls. Very much. Never before, not when she twirled around in her favourite yellow church dress with the wide skirt that stood out like puffing curtains, that used to be mine, not with her head on Mummy's lap, waiting for the baby inside Mummy's belly to kick, smelling faint lavender bath wash and scented powder and lime peel, never before had Theresa felt so loved. And so she picked up and went away.

Before the screaming woke me and the world shifted a little bit to the left, I was standing on the wharf and not even scared of the deep water. There was a boat with a covered space for people to lie down under or sit and eat or play games and music and dance if they liked to get away from the sun or out from beneath the stars. It was about six in the afternoon with the sun just low enough to be behind the boat and just high enough to be right in my eyes. The top deck of the boat was crammed with people I hadn't seen in forever. Mamma Rosario, who I recognized from old photos, was there, and Granny Davis, whose funeral was the first I ever cried at. At the railing was a whole load of little girls in yellow dresses, laughing and waving through the bars. They were blowing me kisses. Nay was there in a coral-pink skirt, and right there in the centre, four heads above everyone else, was Theresa, in a great big straw hat with a brim so wide it shaded her face and shoulders and some other peoples' too. The brim would have been knocking other people in the face if it weren't for how tall she was. I couldn't figure that out either, cause she was three inches shorter than me that morning. If Sweet Mouth had been on that ship, Theresa would have been two heads taller than her.

Theresa was waving too, one long dark arm far above everyone else's. She wore a sapphire dress with buttons down the front and no seams at the side, and she was calling, "See you, Brenda! See you, see you next time!" She sounded so grown, and she wasn't mad that I wasn't waving back. I wanted to, and wanted to run up to the gangplank onto the boat, cause she'd never gone anywhere that far without me before. But my feet were heavy-heavy and my arms couldn't move. She just kept on waving, blowing kisses and waving with one arm. Her other arm was crooked around a huge peacock, sapphire like her dress. I couldn't figure out where she stole or borrowed it from; we never had nothing more exotic than a long-beaked crane in our backyard, and once, some stray Abaco parrots. And she'd never liked birds.

I wondered how she could leave me, and the boat was sailing out, sailing, sailing, sailing, though I never saw anyone pull up the gangplank—never really saw one at all, now that I think. None of those big men, either, who stand on the edge of the boat and loosen it from those green wooden poles on the dock, and push off, then hop into the boat like falling into the water would be nothing. I never saw none of that, and the last thing I could see was Theresa's long arm, and the last thing I knew was that she wasn't mad, but had left me alone and gone with other people. And when I looked down I saw that my ticket for the boat was still in my hand, and while I stared it turned into a sapphire-blue peacock feather with a bone-white eye and I woke in a pant and sat up in the bed and there was a quiet, no crickets or dogs rustling outside. Nothing. And the bed next to me was cool and smooth, the sheets tucked in and empty. Not even a feather left behind.

On August Monday holiday, Emancipation Day, the last little girl left. Most everyone down our street was heading to the beach or some cookout or both. The people in the house in front of ours were rowing, like usual. The man was just in from working late down at the hotel and the woman had been up since before dawn. I didn't hear what they were rowing for, but soon they were slamming doors, and she was wailing, pouring out sorrow like sweet-stink fruit punch from week before last, heaving and wailing almost like a laugh, the way some women cry when no one's doing them anything and they just want attention. Then the back door opened and their older girl came out.

She was a year younger than me, just a bit older than Theresa. I heard her open the car door. I can see her getting into the backseat, leaving the door open, legs dangling out, scratching a bite on her knee. Inside the house, her mother was hollering: "I gone call my mother an' ask her if I could move back home, I can't take it anymore. What you want from me?" Then the yelling stops, and after a while the back door opens, closes quietly. Just as soon as they started, they have stopped and are laughing. I remember thinking that adults are dumb. They walk to the car, the idea of calling her mother's number vanished from the woman's head. They find the girl gone from the car. Not in the front yard, or on the swing out back. Or in the tree. Hasn't come over to see us, or the people next door, or the next or the next, or the next. And there is a wail in the air again, and in it no sweet. Only stink.

The papers lied. The girls were not gone at all. Just relocated. There is no *gone* girls can go in one little community on one little island.

Anyway, what would one person do with all those little girls? Because it wasn't just four. They reported four, but I know there were more. Maybe twenty. Maybe fifty. Maybe a hundred more. I used to hear their voices in their calling hours, after the neighbours had finished their love and the air-conditioning had gone to sleep. On a night without thunder or sirens, they would sing in that silence, throwing their voices up to the ceiling and down into dark corners. Enough for a chorale of little girls freer than wishing can give. Without lessons to learn or rooms to clean, bush to rot under, maggots to feed. They could play all day, all night, mouths full of cookies and songs.

* * *

And they all went so neatly. I imagine them all together, all at one time. Playing twee-lee-lee on the playground in fours, standing in circles, hand overlaid on hand. Someone could come into the playground easy. Someone short and dark, like them, someone with something sweet in her hands. They would scatter at first, like pigeons, then resettle, one by one. The person could ask them if they wanted to learn a new song. Little girls like songs. The little girls could stare, a few nod, a few blink. One could say, *What song you know?*

Come, then, she would say, *when I call, and I'll teach you. It's a song made for sweet things. Sweet things like you.*

Their little hands clapping, voices tinkling and clattering, round glass beads in a jar. This person has them smiling as never before. *Then*, she says, *I will take you on a trip*, her teeth glinting pretty. The little girls begin to skitter and disperse, pigeons again. They settle, this time faster.

You would like a trip, wouldn't you? She smiles and the little girls are thinking of rocking ships and soaring planes and dancing, dancing in clouds.

I dreamed of it often, the song I mean. I could never catch the tune and always woke up to find no one there, just that strange feeling when you're sleeping alone and know someone's in the room with you, pressing down on the foot of the bed.

* * *

There was an arrest. An appearance in court, mothers and sisters hissing and shouting as Sweet Mouth, a small thing who could never wrestle little girls away against their will, was hustled past the crowds, sandwiched between two police officers. She was certainly not as tall as Theresa was in my dream. I am not sure I remember Theresa's real height after all. The woman was thinner too. She looked like she hadn't had a good meal since before the start of the summer. I can't figure out why. Especially with all the rampant fruit. The cookies. All that jam. She must have been so unselfish, brewing plum punch, boiling sugar and fruit, for money and other people, baking little girls cookies while her bones ate her body flesh up in her dusty dark house with plastic-covered furniture no one ever sat in.

She could not have been so bad, especially since they never found any bones or anything. Just bits of fabric in a clearing, from clothes no one recognized, and rows of little folded shirts. And four pairs of small shoes lined up underneath her bed.

The school year after that summer was a hard one. In my class, one seat was empty. For the first month, no one sat next to me on the bus. I wanted it that way. Kept my bag next to me, saving the seat for Theresa. Mothers had it hardest, I guess. Nay's mother had a child in November, a month after Mummy's stillborn. Another girl, Nay's mother had said, when her own baby came. Mummy's hand had tightened around my shoulder. Nay's mother saw it, and started talking about Abe Pratt's amazing comeback at church, which was very old news by then.

In our own house, Mummy began taking down Theresa's dress that used to be mine to iron every morning. It's a shame the dress was yellow and not red, with tips of green and purple strokes, or orange, like the outside and inside of good mangoes. Or peacock blue.

When I see that dress in Mummy's curling fingers, I like to think of Theresa on the boat. How she floats and weaves and bobs above them. I like to think of them all that way, crowded together, playing twee-lee-lee, our great-grandmothers watching over them while Theresa, a full head taller than the rest, waves and blows kisses and I stand on the shore.

It's a shame to think of them any other way. It would waste them.

And why waste little girls?

They are, can be, such nice things.

KIMMISHA THOMAS

Berry
Jamaica

I got a way with me where I always fall for the wrong person, for the wrong reason. Sometimes it's both. Now it's a different brand of fuck-up altogether. This time it's a musician. Sweet Jesus and all the saints, Mam would just go into a state if she found out—after she broke my head.

"Is what wrong now?"

I jumped, worried she knew what I'd been thinking, then shook myself for being stupid.

"Is all right, Mam."

She went back to dipping pieces of hard dough bread into her cornmeal porridge and eating with relish. I was pleased to see her enjoying something. Sometimes I catch her looking at me, a thick crease between her brows. She worried when I was in high school and different from other girls in Greenville. She worried when I was away at uni, afraid of what she heard on the news. Now she worried because I was back and even more different. Other Greenville mothers talked about "mi son-in-law" and "Sophia little one" and normal things that their daughters did. I just went to work, teaching music at Hollifield High. Not that Mam knew that I taught music, nor did I plan on her finding out. And I was not going to stay here and become normal, and bless Mam with a son-in-law and grandkids. I scraped the last bit of porridge from my bowl and stood, looking at my watch. "Leaving now, Mam."

"Yes, me love. Try no late. Every morning, partly, Maude one she run past here 8:00 and school start 8:30. Me sure by time she reach it done late." She kissed her teeth, "I don't know how she keep her job." I left her muttering about the Jamaican government and slackness and went to rinse my mouth and collect my things. I was fortunate to get a taxi quickly, but not so lucky to find myself sitting beside Kathleen. She's the daughter of Mum's friend Maude, and she cannot mind her own damned business.

"Wha you a say, Jackie?" She gave a little laugh. Me early this morning, can't make it look too bad."

"Hmmm," I commented.

"You a go Kineisha wedding Saturday?"

Jesus Christ! "No. Who is she getting married to?"

"You know Neville who drive the dark green robot? You know him last son who use to go Comprehensive?"

I thought hard, "Hmmm, you mean Marlon?" I used to like Marlon one time.

"Yes, him. Bungy them call him."

"Things did a go on here, man."

"Yeah, bare t'ings. A soon you alone." She bumped me with her elbow, grinning like a fool.

Jesus! I gritted my teeth and shook my head as Berry's sweet face flashed across my mind. As my granny often said, *Neither almost nor coulda never kill jackass.*

I looked at the familiar scenery flashing by: Peterson's hardware, with the obsolete blue phone booth still beside it, the Anglican Church on the left, and our Mount Carmel Apostolic a little way down, slap beside Patsy's Hotspot and Bar. There's been changes though. There are new houses and a grocery shop, Tomlinson's One Stop, on the corner where people used to wait for taxis under a huge breadfruit tree. I didn't know any Tomlinsons. The taxi rounded the corner and arrived at my workplace. I paid the driver and got out.

I walked through the gates, prepping myself for the new week. I like my job—when I am not wracked with worry at Mam finding out I teach music. Mam has a story about her twin, Cynthia, who was lost to some mad musician before I was born. Because of Cynthia, mentioning "music" or "musician" in our house is almost the same as if someone tells Mam a gunman is going to break in and kill her tonight. Talk of music and she paces up and down, singing Holy Roller songs, wrapping her arms around her middle, bowing in two like she has an intense bellyache, and groaning. I'm serious, it happens. Strangely, she loves music at church. She calls it *praise*.

I walked into the music room to start preparing for my classes. It was a Monday, which meant "Jazz up your Monday" in Trenton. I'd get to see Berry. My day brightened, but I knew it would pass too slowly.

"Yes, Mam. I have my keys, you can go sleep." I secured the grill and ran through the gate, banging it behind me, not stopping to latch it.

"Jackie! How much time I must tell you—"

"Sorry, Mam!" I called as I ran up the road. Berry teases me that I am twenty-four years old and still can't work up the nerve to tell Mam I am sleeping out.

I waited impatiently for twenty minutes to get a taxi. I was not really late but it felt like it, and Trenton seemed much farther than forty minutes away, especially when I got out of the taxi in Margaret's Bay and had to wait another twenty minutes for a Trenton car. I found myself leaning forward in my seat.

In Trenton, I hurried up the line of bars and clubs to the Cactus. Dancehall music pulsed from the bars and Fire on the Roof was playing Alison Hinds. I rushed on and then I was there, slightly out of breath, in front of the signature neon cactus. The sound of guitar riffs came from inside as the musicians warmed up.

Somebody launched at me when I walked through the door, wrapping me in a tight hug. I recognized Berry's warm smell.

"Is like I could feel you coming," she said, squeezing me tightly.

"Okay, I'm happy to see you too. Don't squeeze the life out of me."

"All right, man. You too soft and dainty."

Once free, I looked around. Nobody was watching us. Maybe they were just pretending.

"Stop it," Berry said, tapping my chin, "nobody nah pree we."

I shrugged. Berry squeezed my hand then ran onto the stage, fiddling with wires and talking to the other players. I admired her lithe form as she moved energetically about. It felt like a candle had been lit in my chest.

The club filled up with regulars as 9:30 drew closer. Marque, a guy I've spoken to before, walked over to me.

"Sexy Jackie, you deserve a drink for that look there." He grinned, looking me up and down.

I felt giddy all of a sudden. I was wearing a soft plum dress that fell to just above my knees, for Berry. "Buy me one then, nuh?"

He raised his eyebrows a little, unprepared for my response. "'Kay. What you want?"

"Surprise me, nuh?"

His brows quirked again. I was surprised at me too.

"All right. You sweet with a little edge. Going bring you suppn to match."

I watched him walk to the bar. Other women were looking at him too, tracking his progress as he came back to me with a Smirnoff Ice Green Apple Bite. I took a swallow, tilting the bottle.

"So, no girlfriend tonight?"

He laughed. "Sanya is not my girlfriend, is my co-worker. What? You interested?"

I laughed a little nervously and felt Berry's eyes on me. I gave her a big smile, then returned to listening to Marque.

"One of my brethren a come link up little more. You think your girlfriend might want us to go check out Dreamz?"

I choked on my drink. My eyes streamed as I coughed, trying to catch my breath. I felt Berry watching me again, but I didn't look at her. "Berry? No, I don't think so. Me and her have plans."

"You can't include we in those plans?"

A laugh bubbled in my chest. The four of us in Berry's bedroom? "No, I don't think so." I started coughing again, trying to squelch the laugh.

"Thank you for coming, ladies and gentlemen. Let's melt your Monday blues with some fine music." That was Brian, who plays bass.

As usual I was drawn to watching Berry's hands and the intensity on her face as she got caught up in the music. "This is praise too, Mam," I whispered, and felt Marque glance at me. I smiled and he smiled back.

After four sets and one bonus "jus cause it's Monday," the club mellowed down to people chatting and drinking and Norah Jones's blue-smoke voice winding through the conversations and rubbing down the edges of too-loud laughs. I was listening to Marque's friend Craig tell how his boss wanted him to work Sundays for no extra pay when Berry came up behind me.

"You look like you comfortable, man." Her breath was mint and cinnamon.

I leaned into her a little. "Guys, I'm going now. Craig, it was nice meeting you." I turned and hooked my arm around Berry's.

"Yeah, nice to meet you too."

"So, I can't get you to change your mind?" Marque asked.

Berry's eyebrow jiggled. I squeezed her arm and laughed. "You guys have guy stuff, we have girl stuff."

Berry's mouth turned up at one corner.

Outside, I swung onto the bike behind her, nuzzling the nape of her neck and breathing in her warm smell. She kicked the bike stand and swung the bike round, then we roared off into the velvet night air. Peeny wallies flickered in the darkness beside the road.

I went in to get ready for bed while Berry locked up the bike. I put my hair into two plaits; nobody would be up to see it when I got home. When she came in, I set the *Gleaner* down and turned to her. She smiled and drew me closer, touching me like I was carefully wrapped silk from across distant seas. I let out my breath in a ragged rush. Berry called me her treasure found, the exact woman she had been waiting for. I've trusted her sureness because she has always been sure—of this, of who she is.

Her hands smoothed over my skin and her mouth hovered over mine, breathing sweetness, building anticipation. When she finally kissed me, I squeezed my eyes shut and arched in response to the violent clenching in my belly. I gave myself over to Berry's sureness. As always, I lost awareness of myself and focused on the sensations we created for each other. At the end, it didn't matter who cried out first or loudest. In this and its effects, we both were sure.

Berry smiled when I said I had to leave. "Little girl," she murmured, and kissed my forehead. "Let me call Trevor." She told me Trevor used to take her to basic school. She won't let anyone else take me home. What if he is unavailable one night? Would she take me home herself? I shivered.

"Are you cold? Come, let me help you dress."

Berry and I first met in a Wendy's. I was in the line when two tall youths who had been checking out the options nudged ahead of me.

"Excuse me?" I tapped the one nearest to me on his shoulder. "I'm sure you do not have a food emergency. I'll thank you to join the line like everybody else."

Somebody behind me sneered something about "dem UPT people, yah." I whipped my head round and saw a tall, lean, dark-skinned girl standing next to a slender young man wearing glasses. Dark eyes danced with amusement above an aquiline nose and a generous, full-lipped mouth. I turned and walked around the youths to place my order. The girl chuckled again as I moved past her when I'd been served. I slammed my tray on a table and stabbed a forefinger in her chest. Her eyes widened.

"For your information, I am from Westmoreland."

"Pardon me, ma'am, for my presumption." She'd laughed happily, showing small, neat teeth.

I found myself smiling back. I *had* been talking in my snotty voice, the one I use to put people in their place. "Sorry, but you know what they say it means to assume."

"Yeah, I do." She stuck out her hand, "Berry Anderson. You want to eat with me and the guys?"

I learned that the youths and the young man were her brothers visiting from Mandeville, and that like me she had only two months left at school, studying music. Strings were her speciality, but she could also play keyboards and piano. She liked jazz and wanted to go to MoBay or somewhere she could play in clubs. As she spoke, I could not help staring at her. It wasn't just her voice, her polished skin, the way her long, tapered fingers picked the food apart. It was those things but also *her*. I thought she was wonderful.

Berry once told me that she had always thought of herself as both female and male. I understand why some men are confused by lesbian logic. I'm confused too. I am sure Berry, so talented and beautiful, always has men lusting after her. I asked one time how she deals with that. She shrugged and said, "I just become their friend. They stay or they leave." She told me her family knows about her. They neither accept nor deny it. "We just *be*, you know?"

I didn't know. I didn't know whether I was gay or not, or whether this was just a phase. But maybe I *did* know, cause I was just *being*, like Berry's family.

Berry says giving me the time I need is no big deal because she gets to enjoy me meanwhile. Still, I wonder if there is some unspoken time frame for making these decisions. Five months after our first kiss, I am still confounded. What happens if I meet someone else?

All the lights were off at home except the one on the verandah. I tried to open the grill and then the front door as quietly as possible. My heart did somersaults when she called my name.

"Yes, Mam?"

"Is three o'clock now, hurry up and go sleep. I don't want you to come like Maude worthless daughter."

"Yes, Mam." I went to my room and closed the door.

Sunday, we have to go to church. Of course. Daddy was a deacon and evangelist here up until the day he died. Away at college, I had gotten used to not see-ing him every day and a small part of my mind tried to pretend that he was only off on one of his longer trips. The day Mam called to say he was dead, after being in the hospital only one night after collapsing at a Wednesday night missionary meeting, was the same night Berry kissed me for the first time. I shook my head, the memories scattered like snowflakes in a toy globe. I looked across at Mam, her head bowed and her lips moving while she prayed, her knuckles shiny as she gripped the backrest of the bench. I wondered how she had taken Dad's death so calmly. I hadn't.

Pastor Laing obviously felt reviving the dwindling population here in Greenville was his personal mission. He wasted no opportunity to urge young people to obey the Lord's will—make honest people of each other and procreate. No matter where the sermon starts, it always ends here. Pity for me there were never many young people around to receive this wisdom. After the service, Mam kept a firm hold on me as she went round greeting her friends. Is like she is friends with the faasest women. There is sage advice on what to do if you were shitting in the bush and saw one of these women coming.

Hear Sister Esther: "Jacqueline, is hiding you been hiding from me? Since you come back I hardly see you. I ask Taneisha if she talk to you, and she didn't even know you come back! You listen good to Pastor Laing? Is true. Young people nowadays have no broughtupcy, too much foreign TV." She shook her head sorrowfully. "Anyway, as Pastor say, there is hope. Unnu just have to take we older heads' advice."

Lord Jesus, if You not busy, stop here. Mam elbowed me and I stopped biting my lip. "Thank you, Sister Esther." We escaped only when I complained I had a splitting headache. In the taxi, Mam said, "Nobody not attacking you, you know, Jackie."

"Hmmm," was all I managed, closing my eyes.

The next day was wet and grey. The kids were fractious at school and my headache would not let up. When the end bell rang I got a taxi home as fast as I could, texted Berry and told her I wasn't coming out. By five o'clock, though, I knew if I didn't do something about the migraine, I would be a dead duck come morning. I cursed my stupidity at not thinking to stop at a pharmacy. They closed at six o'clock, so I could make it if I hurried. I just managed to get in as the guy, jingling a large bunch of keys, was letting someone out. After buying medicine, I was waiting for a taxi when someone grabbed me around the waist.

"Rrrrr!"

I screamed and turned to meet Marque's laughing eyes.

"Gotcha!"

"Jeez! How big man can play so? You frighten the hell outa me!"

"Good thing then, cause an angel not supposed to have hell anywhere near her." He smiled. "You not going to Trenton?"

"No." I held up the prescription bag. "Sick."

"Well, maybe I can hug you better." He pulled me in

for a tight squeeze. After my initial surprise I hugged him back.

"You good?"

"Yes, much better." A taxi pulled up and I got in.

"See you around then."

I watched him walk away. He had a great ass.

It was Heritage Week at school and my headache didn't get much better despite my pill popping. I had to practice with the chorus group, the keyboard and recorder players, and help dance club choose music. I got home late at night, raging at tough-headed, stiff-fingered pickney. Friday night after the heritage concert, all I wanted to do was scrub the week off me and sleep in the next day. I got comfortable under the sheets and my mind ran to Berry. She had said I must be finding something wrong with us because I hadn't set the wheels in motion. "You no must control every-thing, J-baby," she'd chided. Sue me, but I like know-ing what is happening in my life and where it is going. Berry says all I have to do is choose her and everything will be golden.

"I don't want to hurt you, Berry," I whispered to myself. As if on cue, the phone rang.

"You dash me 'way?" Her voice was muffled and I knew she was lying on her stomach. "Or you find new man? A which one?"

Tiredness made my response a little sharp: "You fucking kidding me, right?"

"You tell me."

There was a long silence as I tried to think of a response.

"Anyway, forget that. You want go Port Royal tomorrow?

I bit my lip. How could she just . . . I didn't want to be angry with her. I didn't know how much time we had left. "Yes, I'll come."

"You crying, J-baby? Jus . . . I'm sorry, okay?"

"Okay."

"So . . ."

"Berry, I have to get some rest. I've had a long week, okay?"

"Well . . . okay."

I hung up and pressed my face into the pillow.

The next day was magical. We went to Port Royal and to a fish fry on Lime Cay and watched the sun bleed orange and gold as it fell into the sea. We tried to stretch the magic by going to New Kingston to eat ice cream. Then I was headed home with Berry, and it wasn't Monday. Excitement fizzed and we tried to savour our ice cream and hurry at the same time. We took a short-cut through some buildings to get back to the bike. We were almost there when she pushed me against a wall and then her mouth was on mine in a frenzy of kissing. I reached beneath the hem of her blouse to touch her skin. Then a bottle shattered near my head.

"Yow, unnu leave from here so with that, man!"

I gasped, stunned, and looked over Berry's shoulder to see a small knot of rangy youth approaching.

Berry started toward them and I grabbed her hand.

"Come on, Berry." I pulled her in the other direction.

"Freaky gyal, a dem gyal deh we love!" someone sang out.

Then I was running. I waited for her at the bike.

When we got to her place, I screamed at her stupidity.

She stared at me. "Just stop it, okay? This didn't happen because of you."

I scrubbed my face. "I don't know what the fuck I'm doing!"

"Well, it's time you did, don't it?" Berry cast me a stony look. "J . . . baby, what you intend to do? You know where my heart is, I show you only love. Remember when your father died—"

"Please . . . don't. Don't throw that in my face." Then I was sorry I said it. I knew she must be desperate because she once told me she doesn't like for anyone to feel like they owe her. I could see that I had hurt her. "I think I better leave, okay?"

I turned toward the door but Berry grabbed my shoulders and threw me onto the bed, then knelt astride me. She held my wrists above my head, shaking me hard. "Jackie, how can you jus give up? You haven't seriously given us a try! I am begging you, please, jus love me back!" She kissed me hard, biting my lip. I tasted blood.

I wrenched my wrists free and started to push her away. She bore down harder as if she was trying to fuse our bodies. I lost it. "Get the fuck off me!" I screamed, slapping at her face. She rolled to lie on her back and I jumped up. "I am leaving!"

She caught up with me at the door.

"No! I said I am leaving!" She reached for me and my eyes filled with tears. "Please, Berry, I just want to leave."

She let go of my arm, shaking her head, "Cho, bloodclaat. Maybe you are right. Jus go on." She turned away.

"Berry . . ." I moved to touch her shoulder. Tears were flowing freely now.

She shrugged my hand away. "You say you want leave, so leave."

I stood there, feeling lost. Then I let myself out.

When my father died, somebody called Berry, I don't know why. I had returned from taking Mam's call and was sitting in class, vacant, a roaring in my ears. She came and took me to her flat. It was about nine o'clock in the morning. I'm sure Berry talked to me all through the day, offered things to eat or tried to find out what had happened. She told me later that my phone would ring like crazy and I didn't react. I responded to nothing until she kissed me. I remember staring at her, cocooned in a surreal haze, unable to wrap my mind around what she had done. She'd stood away, watching me. Then I'd launched myself at her. I'd held on to her like I was drowning. I don't know why I did it but the thing is, done is done. I stayed with Berry for one week, coming to life bit by bit, like an Arctic explorer thawing before a fire. She fed me, she kept me clean, she darkened her bedroom and let me lie, a comma curled in the dark. She called Mam, taking the number from my phone on the third day. She stopped Mam from coming to get me, telling her to give me a little time, that I was in a state.

I collapsed again after leaving Berry that Saturday. The driver had to call Mam to pay the fare and help get me into the house. After, I lay in the dark just staring at the wall and listening to songs sung like they had been written just for Berry about me. It wasn't so bad, the numb nothingness. Then Berry sent me a CD.

Jackie,

This song isn't mine but when I sing it I think of you and us. I am ready when you are ready.
Berry

I wasn't surprised that Berry had a beautiful voice. She sang Adele's "Melt My Heart to Stone." The chorus just tore me apart:

And I hear your words that I made up
You say my name like there could be an us
I best tidy up my head, I'm the only one in love . . .

I stayed in bed like this for a few days, then I was

suddenly awake, aware. Mam fed me a bowl of soup but I threw it up. She took me to the doctor the next day, to get tonics to "build me up." She asked no questions. After the consultation, Mam left me in the park to sit in the sun while she went to collect the prescription. I crumpled my sugar bun for the birds and tried to feel real. What was Berry doing now? Was she still angry? Did she miss me too?

"A who this? Where you been hiding, girl?"

I put my hands up against my head. "Quiet, please."

"Hush," Marque lowered his voice. "You sick again, sick fowl?"

I smiled weakly. "Guilty."

"Still sweet though. Is lunchtime, can I stay here and eat my sandwich?"

I gestured to show that he was free to do whatever.

"First, though, there is something I have been longing to find out."

"Yes?" My heart squeezed painfully. Was this about me and Berry?

"Do your lips taste as sweet as they look?"

My breath whooshed out of me. I didn't move. Marque gently held my chin and turned my head. Maybe this was it. Maybe I should see if I could feel what I felt with Berry. His mouth moved closer and I shut my eyes. Nothing; maybe it was too soon. His lips touched mine and they were soft and the kiss was . . . okay. I opened my eyes and pulled away.

"You no waste time at all." Berry's voice could cut ice.

I jumped up, unsteady, and there she was, looking at Marque and me like she could commit murder. I stood there wanting to run to her, my heart beating fast. From the corner of my eye, I could see Mam coming up the path to the gazebo. Berry walked away.

I sighed and Marque turned to look at me. I watched Berry's retreating back. Then I was running, but she was moving too fast and I wasn't strong enough.

"Berry!" I called, but she was nearing the gate now. There was a stitch in my side and I couldn't go any farther. I collapsed onto a bench and wept. "I love you," I whispered, though I knew she couldn't hear me.

Then a pair of shoes came into my line of sight. Berry's purple Converse All Stars.

I wiped my nose with the back of my hand, fresh tears welling. "Stay with me, Berry."

She frowned and shook her head. It was not enough. I stood up and took her hand.

Mam and Marque stood a little way off.

I swallowed and squeezed Berry's hand. She squeezed back.

"Mam, this is Berry. My girlfriend."

Her brow furrowed. "Your friend?"

"Her girlfriend," Marque said, shaking his head a little.

I hugged Berry hard, leaning into her. "I can't promise forever," I said.

"That's okay," she hugged me back, "we'll work it out."

We looked at Mam, her face still a picture of puzzlement, and Marque, his expression cryptic. Yes, we would have to work it out.

KEVIN JARED HOSEIN

The Monkey Trap
Trinidad & Tobago

Talon sat by the gully at the back of his house with a collection of crumpled leaves in his palm. He had been trying to fashion a boat out of each one, just as Sana had shown him a couple days before with a piece of newspaper, but the leaves snapped with each bend and fold.

He scratched the sparse white hairs lining his ears. Sweat and muck marred his white cotton vest, and he had recently soiled his underpants. A light evening wind blew the foul scent into the backwoods.

A devotional Hindi hymn played from his house upstairs. Talon figured that Sana was up in her room. Blending in with the hymn was Harry Belafonte's voice faintly playing from another window:

Don't know what to say de monkey won't do
Well, I drink gin, monkey drink gin too

Don't know what to say de monkey won't do . . .

Talon inspected the green leafy pulp on his palm and peered at two bachacs busily chewing the stems. He grunted, crushing the leaves in his fist, and blew the mush into the water. He dusted his palms off. Then he heard a rustling. He raised his bushy eyebrows and scanned the thicket ahead of him, mumbling, "That blasted monkey come again?"

Still sitting, he raised his knees against his chest. He moved his hand and accidentally knocked a broken Carib bottle into the gully. It rolled along the sandstone, clinking.

The monkey probably hear that. Talon gritted his teeth. His toes curled, scooping up some dirt beneath his overgrown nails. He scooted forward into the gully, the filthy water now over his toes, his soles pressing into the green slime along its edge.

He scratched the stubble on his cheek as he listened to the rustling shrubs and looked hard for the hairy figure that must be creeping through the bush.

He squinted.

From the house the song bridge had kicked in, drums and brass carried by the dusk breeze. The bushes rustled again; Talon was sure it was the monkey.

His ears pricked up as the monkey groaned.

"Daddy, you mess yourself again!" a voice called out from behind him. He spun around, now looking at his daughter's heaving bodice. Then he turned back to peer at the hedge. Nothing. She had scared the monkey off.

"Girl." Talon mumbled when he spoke, as if he had food in his mouth. "Girl, look, look, the monkey there in the bush."

Sana sucked her teeth. She stooped down and hooked her arm under his shoulder. With a tug, she got him to his feet. "It have no monkey in the bush, Daddy," she said with a sigh, and shook her head. "No monkey does live around here. How much times I have to tell you that?"

She led Talon to a small basin she had set up at the side of the house, screened by three tall sheets of rusted metal and a tattered drape. She had left the water to run and the basin was already half full.

She produced a black plastic garbage bag and set it aside.

"But I see it, I see it," Talon chanted as Sana helped him undress. A long shiny brown scar, the result of a cutlass slash from a bandit fifteen years ago, stood prominent on his chest. Sana put on a pair of gardening gloves and slid his boxers off, turning away as she did.

She wondered if he recognised her anymore. For a few weeks now he had stopped calling her by her name. He used to say, in a comforting singsong manner, *Sana, dahlin, Sana, little la-a-dy,* whenever he needed her. It upset her, too, that over the last week he had become incontinent.

She slid her thumb along the scar, remembering the night he had tried to defend her and her deceased mother from two criminals. They had made off with the TV set and some golden bangles, family heirlooms, but the two women were unharmed. Talon was left splayed on the bedroom floor, struggling for breath, soaked in blood. They had never been able to get the bloodstain out of the thick cerise carpeting.

She wondered if he remembered that.

She pinched the dirty underwear between her fingers, dropped it into the garbage bag, tied a double knot, and tossed it through the drape.

"What if the monkey come back?" Talon asked.

Sana tied her shoulder-length hair into a ponytail and leaned against the edge of the basin, bowing her head. She muttered a prayer quickly. She looked at him with warm eyes, as she formed a lather on the sponge. She said, "I want you to stay inside from now on. I can't have you wanderin bout the place when I gone to work. I dunno how you gone and pick up that nasty habit."

"No wanderin?"

His sullen tone made her brow pucker. "You have your radio," she added. "You remember how to turn the station? You remember how to turn on the TV?"

He was silent.

"I'll show you again after you bathe."

"Okay."

The next day, Sana left some sandwiches for him on the

kitchen counter and covered them with a few napkins. But Talon had no appetite for them. He took one of the sandwiches and set it by the gully, then crept back to the house and went upstairs. He parted the curtains and stared down. *Where that monkey? Maybe monkey ain't like bologna.*

He went to the tiny fruit tub Sana kept under the table and rummaged through the oranges, grapes, and three different types of mango. Not what he was looking for. He sucked his teeth and scratched his head. He opened the other cupboards and searched through the wares. Impatient, he began hurling them across the room.

By the time he was finished with the top cupboards, shards of terra-cotta, porcelain, and glass lay strewn across the kitchen floor.

He then fumbled through the refrigerator, throwing aside all the celery and tomatoes and ripping apart a small seasoned chicken Sana had intended to cook for them the following day. He bit his tongue and grimaced. He ran to the kitchen window and looked out again. The sandwich was still there.

Of course, it was not going anywhere. Monkeys would not be interested in meat.

Talon bounded back upstairs, knocking over the radio on the counter. It broke as it fell. He opened Sana's closets, full of her work clothes and her saris. He tore them off the hangers and flung them on the floor and the bed. He pulled the drawers open until they came off their runners. He fumbled through her lingerie, searching, then pitching them under the bed. He swept his arm through the assortment of Sana's makeup and fragrances, sliding them off the dresser.

He opened a little box. It played a melody, like a miniature calliope. He stared at the tiny ballerina figurine twirling in the box, a dazed smirk on its plastic face.

The tune stopped.

He closed the box, then opened it again and listened to the melody once more. He put the box back on the dresser, sat on the edge of the bed, and muttered, "Where them figs could be?"

He made his way downstairs and decided not to pass through the kitchen, to avoid having his feet cut by the splintered wares. He slipped on his rubber flip-flops from the porch, passed around the house, and went back to the gully.

The sandwich was still there, now infested with ants.

He stood by the gully and glared into the thicket. It rustled again. The monkey was there, curling its tail at him. If only he had those bananas. The thought crossed his mind to go to the market to buy some. But he had no time for that. No money either. And the monkey would escape by then!

He went to the kitchen door and picked up a broom lying against it. He unscrewed the brush head and jabbed the air with the broomstick like a spear. He headed outside and crossed the gully, tiptoeing across the smooth rocks, pressing the stick against the bottom to keep his balance. He clambered up the muddy bank, breathing heavily in the hot, humid air.

The bushes rustled again and he could hear a low murmur and chatter. He parted the bushes with the broomstick. He saw the monkey's head, fidgeting silently. He grinned, his eyes opened wide, and lifted the broomstick above his head. With one swift blow, the monkey fell unconscious.

Sana came home early from work that day. Her heart beat violently as she entered the house and noticed the chips of glass and ceramic on the kitchen floor. Her first thought was that they had been robbed again. She saw the broken radio. She dashed upstairs to find her rummaged closets. Her saris were scattered across the bedroom carpet. Where was her father?

Then she heard a yelping coming from outside. She peeked through the window and saw her father kneeling by the old wooden dog kennel, last used when they had owned a pothound years ago.

She scrambled downstairs.

As she approached, her father looked at her with pride in his eyes. She had not seen his eyes twinkle like that in years. "Dahlin," he said, sticking his chest out, "I tell you it had a monkey."

Sana's jaw dropped. In the dog kennel was not a monkey but Akeel, a little boy from the village. He had been packed into the kennel, too afraid to speak, too afraid to scream. A trickle of dried blood was clotted on his right eyebrow. He peered up at Sana, blinking his watery eyes.

As Sana began to undo the latch, Talon exclaimed, "But the monkey will get out, girl!"

Sana paused. Her eyes had begun to get hot as she stared at Akeel. She wiped her nose with her sleeve and mouthed to the little boy, "Stay here," and clasped Talon's arm.

"Do you know Akeel, Daddy?" Sana asked, leading him back into the house.

"The monkey friends might come lookin for him, girl. We need to make market and get a basket of fig."

Sana took a deep breath, then nodded slowly and wiped her brow with her sleeve. "In the morning, we could do that . . . It have a big crocus bag lyin around near the washroom there. We could fill that up. Right up."

She escorted him up the stairs as Talon told her, "We have to get the green ones too."

"Why the green?"

"So they could yellow if the other monkeys takin too long to come."

Sana nodded again. She led him into the bedroom and made him sit on the bed. "Daddy," she began, her voice sweet and slow as molasses, "how bout if we just leave the monkeys alone? I don't think they goin to do we anything."

"No, no. Them monkeys is pests. They goin to pester the whole village."

Sana covered her face. He had not sounded as strong and stern for years. She took another deep breath and gave Talon a hug. His arms hung limp as she squeezed him. "No chance at all," she whispered in his ear, her voice breaking.

"Girl, you just don't understand," he said gruffly.

She buried her face against the crook of his shoulder. "It might have some men comin tomorrow to move you away. People might say some nasty things from now bout you." She swallowed hard. "And me."

He didn't speak, he just nodded.

Sana cleared her throat. "Is just that some people here like the monkeys, and they movin everybody who don't like the monkeys to a different spot."

"Them mad or what? Why them want them monkeys around?"

With her palms pressed against his shoulders, she kissed his cheek, his beard grazing her lips. "You work hard today. I need you to take a rest now. I going downstairs for a while." She hugged him again and left the room, locking the door.

When she went back to the kennel, Akeel's eyes grew wide, but he said nothing. As she undid the latch, she broke down in tears. "Akeel, please don't tell anybody what happen here today."

He shook his head.

While mimicking him nervously, she asked, "What

does that mean? Does that mean you going to tell?"

She released the latch, opened the kennel door, and pulled him out. He was shaking; his knees wobbled as he blinked at the sky.

"Lemme dress that cut," she said. "We can't leave that so."

He backed away from her.

"Come. I have food inside too. Lemme give you something to eat."

He took another step back.

"Akeel, please," she whispered.

The boy darted off.

The next day, the authorities came in their white coats and packed Talon into a van. When they arrived, he was listening to the music box. All the neighbours had come out to watch. Sana saw their cold stares as she hugged her father goodbye. Akeel's mother shook her head. As Sana returned to the house, the villagers turned their backs on her.

She packed her clothes back into her closets and ironed her saris. She opened the music box and, as the tune played, as the ballerina twirled, she got on her knees and tried yet again to scrub the old blood off the bedroom carpet. No matter how much she tried, she just could not get it out of the fibres.

GARFIELD ELLIS

Father, Father
Jamaica

Call *your father now, nuh!*
My breath is hot in my nostrils, tears of anger burn my eyes as I run, and the blood drips down my face where a stone has burst my head.

Call your father now, nuh!

There are three boys after me.

One, I could beat easily. Two, I could take a chance and stand and fight. But three is too much. They have my knapsack. I had to leave it as the ugly one grabbed it, twisting my neck as he pulled at it to try to stop me. But I swivelled hard and left it in his hand. Dirt splatters from a wall in front of me as a rock is thrown at my head. I run and zigzag through the narrow lane.

Call your father now, nuh!

"Touch me," I had said, "lay one finger on me or any of my friends, and I will call my father to lock you up and make them run you family out of the dirty canefield hut you live in. My father is in charge of all canefields from here to Clarendon. Touch me—no, open your mouth—and I call my father and you and all your ugly family will turn beggars."

A shove had gone with that threat. Little boy in torn khaki was at the end of that shove, standing there with his friend, trying to hustle money from us, John and me. Saying how he liked my shoes. Young snarling dirty boys who hardly passed through the school gate except to get their names noted on the register once or twice a week. Sullen boys, dirty boys with downturned eyes, hating school as much as school hated them. Maybe because they smelled so much . . . too poor to change their clothes or bathe anywhere except the irrigation canal that fed the canefields. Their skin was as chalky and scaly as fish left to die in the sun. Always there, standing at the gate, intimidating those they could, fondling the girls, and threatening those they think are soft.

But I would not be soft. I stood up to them.

"You never had to insult them so, we could just walk them out," John said.

"I never insult them—I just tell them the truth."

"But we could a just walk them out. Leave them alone. Them will kill you, those people have gun."

"Cho, they don't want me to call my father."

Now they chase me down a lane that leads to a place I don't know. *And where is John? Disappeared the moment he saw them. Isn't he the one who got me into this? Isn't he the one I defended when I took them on? Isn't he the one I offered to follow home though it was miles out of my way because he was scared to pass alone through the area where these dirty ugly boys live? Now I'm alone, far from home and even farther from the safety of the school crowd where I took them on.*

There is no shelter here in Portmore, just the sun beating down on this concrete gully with its intermittent tracks of dirt. I am running from one strange lane to another. I don't know where I am going and I am running out of breath.

Call your father now, nuh!

I wish I could call him; I wish he would come. Drive his big car, park it at the end of the alley down which my tired legs now falter, open his arms to my charge while lifting his larger-than-life self to its full height, raising his hand like Moses pushing back the sea . . . like the great defender I boast him to be. *Touch my big son, just touch one hair on his head, if you think you're bad.*

But I am alone. I have no father to rescue me.

Call your father now, nuh!

I am tired. The open fences, dirty houses, are all part of one hot, hazy blur around me.

I cannot go much farther.

A large lamppost looms. It is a crossroad with an alleyway to the left and right. I brace myself and swing right. The feet behind me are closer and seem multiplied in my ears. I swerve around the corner, and before me are houses on every side. Then there is a cul-de-sac with a narrow lane feeding off to the left; it is the only escape from this box that traps me. But standing there is a snarling boy with a knife in his hands. I have been herded into a dead end.

I pull up quickly, but lose my footing and fall, skating in the dust on the seat of my pants till my backside burns from the gravel.

Call your father now, nuh!

Anytime you need me, he had said, *just call. Just call, man, and I will come.* I now realise how deceitful a promise that had been, for how can I call him? How do I know where he is at any time of day, and even if I did, by what means would I reach him? How stupid I was to believe that I could call. . . and even more stupid to think that he would come.

Call your father.

Call me when you ready! Though he knows I have no way to do so. *I will come when you want,* though he knows he will never come, will never be there when I want. Nor will he be there when I return home after I have been beaten.

Big son, my big son.

Big son! Maybe after this, when I am dead, he will come. Maybe then he will find me, me who he has neglected. Big son! Yes, big son in the dust now, faced down by a knife and three cowards. Maybe when I am dead, maybe then. Someone else will call and then he will have no choice but to come. Someone will call and tell him, *Your big son dead, man . . .* Then he will come.

Then he will know . . . that I wanted him, that I called and he did not come.

"Call your father now, nuh!" Big ugly, bulky boy, whose name I do not know, on the right edge of the circle of three that converge on me. "Your father not coming now? So I live in a shack, I live in a canefield . . . so your father goin chase me out like a dog? Your father is a bad man? You call him? I don't see him. Call him now, nuh."

He has spoken my thoughts into the hot day. He should not have done that. My hatred for my father is my own. So I choose him. I choose him now, that boy of sixteen years or so, two years older than me, a head and a half taller, big and broad like a mature footballer, with a knife in his hand as long as my arm and a mocking snarl on his face, I choose him this day to die with.

I am at his throat, from crouching in the dust, through the air so fast it is as if the earth has tilted to meet his slamming back. There is no strategy to the attack, no form to the madness. I am an animal broken loose, teeth bared, biting, sinking into dirty flesh till blood runs down my face. Head butting, stiff arms tightening around an ugly thick neck, knees pumping, kicking, legs flaying. Angry animal gurgling and savage grunts coming from me. It is expelling something deep and deadly in this dirty place, on this hot dusty road. I shall vomit everything here and now, for I shall not return from this place. I shall not return to be anything he wants—not to ambition and good grades, not to school and vacant parent-teacher chairs, or the empty stands when I compete in athletics. I shall not return to a lonely home and a mother who tells me to turn the cheek all the time, nor to the empty spaces of my room and the echoes of empty promises and a voice so strong, a smile so sweet, and face so godly. I shall not return from this place. I shall kill him now. I shall die right here with him, with this ugly, thick, smelly person. I shall kill him now and die right here in the hot dust of a strange and ugly street. Right here, right now, I shall die for him; I shall die with him . . . I with this empty space that I see is my father.

Call your father now. Leave me alone, police people. I do not want to know I almost killed him.

Call your father now. Leave me alone, hospital people. Leave the knife right there buried in my shoulder.

Call your father now. Leave me alone, mother people. I do not know, I cannot tell what is wrong with me.

Call your father now. Leave me alone, father people. Let the scowl drop from your face, for I called and you did not come. I wanted you and you were not there. You are never there when I need you! Leave me alone, father . . . for when I call, when I need you . . . you do not come.

Call your father now, nuh! No, I will not call him. I have no voice to call. I am alone and I am empty . . . I have no one to call . . . I have no father to call . . . I have no one. . . I am alone . . . let me die alone . . . I have no one . . . I have no father.

Call your father, call your father, call your father . . .
Father . . . Father . . . Father!

ABOUT THE CONTRIBUTORS

No Author Photo

EZEKEL ALAN'S debut novel, *Disposable People*, was awarded the 2013 Commonwealth Book Prize Regional Award for the Caribbean. A native of Jamaica, he works as an international consultant in Asia, where he is currently based with his wife and kids, has a good, reliable dog, and enjoys a satisfyingly abundant supply of sweet, juicy mangoes.

Rattan Jadoo

KEVIN BALDEOSINGH is a journalist and author. His novels include *The Autobiography of Paras P.* (Heinemann Caribbean Writers Series, 1996); *Virgin's Triangle* (Heinemann Caribbean Writers Series, 1997); and *The Ten Incarnations of Adam Avatar* (Peepal Tree Press, 2005). In 2011, *Caribbean History for CSEC*, a textbook coauthored with historian Dr. Radica Mahase, was published by Oxford University Press.

Rachelle Gray, GrayWorks Media

HEATHER BARKER moved to Barbados from the UK as a child. Issues of identity and belonging have shaped her writing. In 2010 she was a finalist in Barbados' foremost literary prize, the Frank Collymore Literary Endowment, and in 2008 she received the George Lamming Prize for Literary Excellence for the short story "Letter to Dee." Barker is a professional communicator by day and a world traveller at heart. For more information, visit www.clearlycontent.net.

GARFIELD ELLIS is a two-time James Michener Fellow to the Caribbean Writers Institute (1992, 1993), two-time winner of the Una Marson Prize for Adult Literature (1997, 2000) and the Canute A. Brodhurst Prize for Short Fiction (2000, 2005), and also won the 1990 Heinemann/Lifestyle Short Story Competition. He is the author of *Flaming Hearts and Other Stories, Wake Rasta and Other Stories, Such As I Have, For Nothing at All,* and *Till I'm Laid to Rest.*

Emile Hill

JOANNE C. HILLHOUSE is the Antiguan and Barbudan author of *The Boy from Willow Bend, Dancing Nude in the Moonlight, Oh Gad!,* and *Fish Outta Water.* Her writing has appeared in the collections *In the Black; So the Nailhead Bend, So the Story End;* and *For Women: In Tribute to Nina Simone;* and in the journals *Caribbean Writer, Columbia Review, Calabash, MaComère, Poui,* and others. "Amelia" was short-listed in the 2013 *Small Axe* Literary Competition. Visit jhohadli.wordpress.com for more details.

KEVIN JARED HOSEIN is a poet, writer, and teacher in Trinidad and Tobago, and a graduate of the University of the West Indies. He illustrated and published his first book, *Littletown Secrets*, in 2013. His poem "The Wait Is So, So Long" was adapted into a short film which was awarded a Gold Key at the New York–based Scholastic Art & Writing Awards. His story in this volume was also short-listed in the 2013 *Small Axe* Literary Competition.

BARBARA JENKINS is a Trinidadian whose short fiction has won many awards, including the Commonwealth Short Story Prize, Caribbean region, the *Wasafiri* New Writing Prize, the *Small Axe* Literary Competition, and the inaugural Hollick Arvon Caribbean Writers Prize in 2013. Her debut story collection, *Sic Transit Wagon*, was published by Peepal Tree Press in 2013. She spends her days reading, writing, and swimming at Macqueripe Bay.

IVORY KELLY is the author of *Point of Order: Poetry and Prose* (Ramos Publishing, 2009). Her works have also appeared in several Belizean anthologies, including *The Alchemy of Words*, Vol. 2 (2008); *Treasures of a Century* (2005); *Memories, Dreams, and Nightmares*, Vol. 1 (2002); and *She* (2001). Kelly grew up in Sittee River Village, Belize. She currently lives in Belmopan and teaches in the English department at the University of Belize.

SHARON LEACH'S fiction has been anthologized in publications such as *Kunapipi: Journal of Postcolonial Writing*; *Iron Balloons: Hit Fiction from Jamaica's Calabash Writer's Workshop*; *Stories from Blue Latitudes: Caribbean Women Writers at Home and Abroad*, the *Jamaica Journal*, *Caribbean Writing Today*, *Calabash*, and *Afrobeat*. Her first book, *What You Can't Tell Him: Stories*, was published in 2006. A second collection of stories is forthcoming from Peepal Tree Press.

JANICE LYNN MATHER is a Bahamian writer who holds an MFA from the University of British Columbia, and has published in journals and anthologies such as *Tongues of the Ocean*, *A Sudden and Violent Change*, and *We Have a Voice*. Her writing has been short-listed in the 2011 *Small Axe* Literary Competition and for the 2012 and 2013 Commonwealth Short Story Prize. She lives in Vancouver, BC, but will always be a Nassau gal.

Ross Millar

SHARON MILLAR is a graduate of the Lesley University MFA program. She was the winner of the 2012 *Small Axe* Literary Competition and the co-winner of the 2013 Commonwealth Short Story Prize. Her work has appeared on several short lists including the inaugural 2013 Hollick Arvon Caribbean Writers Prize for Fiction. She lives in Port of Spain, Trinidad, with her husband and daughter.

Caroline Forbes

OLIVE SENIOR is an award-winning Jamaican poet, novelist, and short story writer currently living in Canada. Her novel *Summer Lightning* won the Commonwealth Writers Prize, and her poetry collection *over the roofs of the world* was short-listed for Canada's Governor General's Literary Award and Cuba's Casa de las Américas Prize. Her nonfiction works on Caribbean culture include the *A–Z of Jamaican Heritage*, *Working Miracles*, and *The Encyclopedia of Jamaican Heritage*.

KIMMISHA THOMAS is a native of Ocho Rios, Jamaica. A lover of words and language since childhood, she has studied creative writing in various classes and workshops. Thomas has published short fiction and poetry in the *Jamaica Gleaner*'s Arts pages and the *Observer*'s Bookends. For four years she worked to instill her passion for words in Jamaican children, and currently teaches in Japan.

DWIGHT THOMPSON is a Jamaican working in Japan as an English teacher. His work has appeared in the *Montego Bay Western Mirror* and *Caribbean Writer,* where he won the Charlotte and Isidor Paiewonsky Prize. One of his stories was also short-listed for a prize in the 2012 *Small Axe* Literary Competition.